Herbie Brennan

Illustrated by The Maltings Partnership

First published in 2006 by Faber and Faber Limited
3 Queen Square, London WC1N 3AU

Editorial management: Paula Borton
Designed by Planet Creative Ltd
Printed in England by Bookmarque Ltd

A CIP record for this book is available from the British Library

ISBN 0571 223141

2 4 6 8 10 9 7 5 3 1

Contents

To Fintan. A small celebration of many years of friendship.

What if...

... you can't trust your teachers? What if you can't believe your parents?

What if...

... the things you know for sure are just plain wrong?

What if...

... scientists sometimes just make up the answers?

What if...

... the world is not the way you think it is? What if history is all lies? What if the stuff they tell you is impossible keeps happening every day?

What if…

…Atlantis once existed?… parallel worlds are real… you have powers beyond your wildest dreams?

What if…

… time travel is *already* happening?

Chapter 1

Paradoxes of Time

Do you know *The Time Machine?* You may have read the book (by H. G. Wells) or maybe seen the movie – Hollywood made at least two versions to my knowledge. It described how a Victorian inventor created a marvellous machine full of cogs and wheels and whirligigs that let you dial a date, set the engine going and travel backwards or forwards in time.

Time travel opens up some fascinating possibilities ... including time tourism. The sci-fi writer Ray Bradbury explored that theme, with a particularly nasty twist, in his short story *The Sound of Thunder.* The story dealt with Time Safaris Inc., an organisation that specialised in carrying hunters back to the age of the dinosaurs where they could have the thrill of shooting a *Tyrannosaurus Rex.*

Bradbury went beyond simple adventure by examining a big problem with time travel: any action taken in the past might well make changes in the future. So tourists in a time safari were strictly required to remain on a specially-constructed floating platform and shoot only prey that had been particularly chosen for them. Furthermore, the Tyrannosaur they were hunting was scheduled to die soon anyway, killed by a falling tree. But as in all good stories, something went wrong. One of the party, a nervous man, was so terrified by the appearance of the dinosaur that he stepped off the floating platform and fled, blundering his way through the undergrowth.

By the time the dinosaur was shot and the panicked party member dragged back to the platform, the damage was done. The leader of the safari noticed the broken body of a tiny butterfly crushed by the runaway's boot. Just a single, insignificant insect, but the effects of its death reached down the ages until, when the party returned to their own era, they found that the kind and tolerant culture they'd left had been replaced by a harsh regime that promptly jailed them for illegal time travelling.

The idea of tinkering with the past in order to change the future has always proved fascinating. It was the theme of the *Terminator* movies starring Arnold Schwarzenegger, all of which featured individuals sent back in time on missions designed to influence the future/present. I even made use of it myself, years ago, in a science fiction story called *Time Lord,* which described what appeared to be a time traveller intent on the assassination of Adolf Hitler.

The assassination of Adolf Hitler features frequently in discussions about time travel which

spotlight a paradox (a fact or situation that seems to contradict itself). Consider the following: you, a time traveller, read a harrowing account of the slaughter during the Second World War. Being a decent sort, you decide to travel back to 1938 and assassinate Hitler before he has a chance to start the conflict.

Your mission is a stunning success. You shoot the Fuhrer with a sniper rifle during a Nuremberg Rally and make your escape before his startled guards can react. With Hitler dead, the invasion of Poland never takes place and consequently there is no Second World War. But since there was no Second World War, you could not read an account of the slaughter and so you would never think of going back in time to assassinate Hitler...

If you follow that one through, you end up in a sort of closed loop in which the World War caused you to kill Hitler which stopped World War II which caused you not to kill Hitler which caused World War II which caused you to kill Hitler which ... and so on, more or less forever.

A Russian physicist working on the mathematics of time has announced his calculations show that while time travel is theoretically possible, time paradoxes are not. Our current understanding of time seems to suggest that while the future might be changed by making changes in the past, the energy required to create a major paradox – like the assassination of Hitler described in this chapter – exceeds the total energy available in the universe.

Thus, if the calculations are accurate, you can in theory travel through time, but are prevented from creating time loops or directly harming yourself by actions like murdering your mother before she had a chance to give birth to you.

The fantasy writer Michael Moorcock produced a thought-provoking variation on the theme in his novel *Ecce Homo.* This told the story of a time traveller who was so fascinated by the impact of religion on human culture that he decided to return to Palestine at an era that would allow him to witness the crucifixion of Jesus Christ.

In order not to influence the past, he equipped himself by learning the language of the time – Aramaic – and brought clothing that would allow him to blend in with the local people. The trip was successful and he carefully hid his time machine away in a cave. But when he started asking questions about Christ and His teachings, he was arrested by the Romans as a troublemaker and then crucified ... thus creating the very incident that caused him to travel back in time in the first place.

But the Hitler business and Michael Moorcock's ingenious tale are nothing compared to some of the *really* tricky paradoxes time travel could throw up. For example, what happens if your time travel mission is to kill your own grandmother?

You have to watch the timing very carefully, because if that mission succeeds before your grandmother has given birth to your mother, then your mother will never be born. And if your mother will never be born, then neither will you, so you couldn't go back in time to kill your own grandmother.

It could get worse. Suppose at the age of 16 you travel back in time and meet up with the girl of your dreams, also 16 years old. You start going out together and a couple of years later you get married and start a family. It's only then you discover that you've married the woman who became your mother, with the result that you are now your own father. Ouch!!

I'm not saying these situations are particularly likely, but the point is if anybody ever gets around to inventing time travel, they all become *possible*[1].

Which is why, I suppose, so many philosophers – and quite a few scientists – have decided time travel simply can't happen. Unfortunately, the evidence is against them.

1. Unless the calculations of the Russian physicist prove correct. See the panel in this chapter for details.

Chapter 2

The Weird Experience of Mrs Jane O'Neill

Something peculiar happened to Jane O'Neill in 1973. The Cambridge schoolteacher was driving on a busy road when she witnessed a horrific accident. Just ahead of her, a car smashed into a packed coach, badly damaging both vehicles.

Mrs O'Neill ran to help. As she was the first person on the scene, she started to pull people from the wreckage. In moments, her hands were covered in blood, but she worked on, then waited by the roadside with the injured until the ambulances arrived. After that, she drove to London to pick up a friend at the airport.

On the way home again much later that evening, the weirdness started. In vivid flashes, Mrs O'Neill

began to see the dreadful injuries of the passengers all over again. She managed to get home safely, but the flashbacks continued day after day. Unusually for her, she found she was losing sleep, then stopped sleeping altogether. Her health began to deteriorate and, in desperation, she went to see her doctor. He told her she was suffering from shock and suggested she take time off work to recover. Mrs O'Neill stayed away from school for fully five weeks and started to feel a little better, but her strange experience was far from over.

Half term rolled around and a friend named Shirley invited her to take a break in Shirley's cottage in Norfolk. Jane O'Neill readily agreed, but the country air did nothing to stop the flashbacks – except that now they were no longer flashbacks. Very different scenes had begun to replace the disturbing visions of the accident.

On one occasion, Mrs O'Neill saw two figures walking through trees beside a lake and recognised one of them (without knowing how) as Margaret Roper, a daughter of Sir Thomas More, the English

lawyer, scholar and saint who was beheaded for treason by Henry VIII. Another time, she told her friend Shirley that she'd just seen her in the galleys. Shirley surprised her by remarking that her ancestors were Huguenots (French protestants) who had been persecuted and sent to the galleys.

These experiences took the form of vivid pictures which lasted no more than a few seconds, but held Mrs O'Neill's attention utterly. There seemed to be no link between her visions and some of them failed to make very much sense – on one occasion, for example, she simply saw a horse and what looked like an armadillo facing up to one another. But in every case, the visions exhausted her.

Unpleasant though they were, these experiences were at least explicable. In fact, they had already been explained by her doctor. As any psychologist would confirm, a severe shock like witnessing the bloody accident, could easily trigger hallucinations. At first these were directly related to the accident itself. Later, as the emotional impact died down, they changed to historical visions, probably based on something she'd read, or complete fantasies like

the stand-off between the armadillo and the horse. But then, about eight weeks after the accident, Mrs O'Neill visited Fotheringhay Church.

Fotheringhay Church in Northamptonshire is the place where Mary Queen of Scots was executed. When Jane O'Neill visited in 1974, her attention was taken by a picture of the crucifixion behind the altar. In particular, she studied the ornamental arch above the picture. There was a dove carved underneath it, its outstretched wings following the curve of the arch.

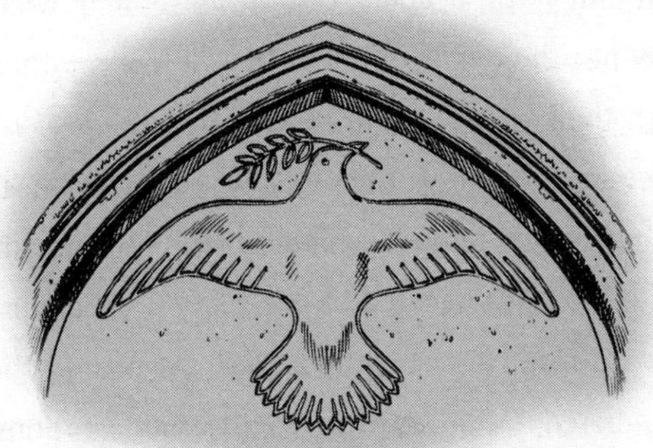

The trip was made with her friend Shirley – the same friend who invited her to the Norfolk cottage. They were together a few hours later in their hotel room when something Shirley said reminded Jane about the arch and she mentioned the picture. Shirley looked at her blankly: *she* had seen no picture in the church.

This started to prey on Jane O'Neill's mind. She decided to ask the vicar and phoned the local post office for his number. It turned out there hadn't been a vicar in the parish for three years, but the postmistress arranged flowers in the church every Sunday ... and insisted there were no proper pictures in it anywhere. The only thing she could think of was the dove on a board behind the altar – quite clearly not the crucifixion painting Jane had seen.

With their visit drawing to a close, there was no chance for the two women to return to the church, but the mystery nagged at Jane O'Neill until, a year later, the friends decided to come back.

The outside of the church was exactly as she remembered it, but when she went inside she knew at once she was in a different building. It was much smaller than the Fotheringhay she'd visited before. There was no painting of the crucifixion. And even the dove behind the altar was quite different to the

one she'd seen earlier. Shortly afterwards, she discovered the church had a reputation for being haunted. People reported hearing music coming from inside while the building was empty. Furthermore, it was a very old-style music, of the type that was popular when Plantagenet kings ruled England about 800 years ago.

Astounded and disturbed, Mrs O'Neill got in touch with a Northamptonshire historian, who told her that the original Fotheringhay Church had been pulled down in 1553 and the present building erected on the site. Further research confirmed something unbelievable. The church Mrs O'Neill had entered in 1973 seemed to be the one that had been demolished more than 400 years previously. When the author Colin Wilson contacted Mrs O'Neill as part of an investigation into the paranormal, she told him she thought she might have known the church in a previous lifetime and her experience was some sort of visionary memory. But there's a simpler explanation. It may be that Jane O'Neill travelled back in time.

Chapter 3

Time-Travelling Teachers

More than 70 years before the weird events at Fotheringhay, another English schoolteacher had an even more spectacular time-travel experience ... and, unlike Jane O'Neill, she was not alone.

The schoolteacher in question was Miss Charlotte Anne Elizabeth Moberly, Principal of St Hugh's Hall at the University of Oxford. In 1901, the year Queen Victoria died, she happened to meet Miss Eleanor Frances Jourdain, a teacher who had founded her own girl's school in Watford. Miss Moberly was impressed. So impressed she actually offered Miss Jourdain the post of Vice-Principal at St Hugh's. Miss Jourdain responded by inviting Miss Moberly to stay with her at her flat in Paris to see how they got on together. So on a hot August day, the two women set off for a three-week holiday in France.

Since they were both interested in history, they decided to visit historical sites in and around Paris. Top of their agenda was the Palace of Versailles, only a 20-minute train ride from the city. On August 10, they made that journey ... and became a little part of history themselves. There was a lot to see at the Palace of Versailles. The original building, erected in 1634, was a hunting lodge for Louis XIII, but his successor, Louis XIV, transformed it into an immense, extravagant complex surrounded by ornate English and French gardens.

It became the official seat of the French Court in 1682 but was abandoned after the death of Louis XIV in 1715. But just seven years later it again became the royal residence and further additions were made by kings Louis XV and XVI. The whole place was nearly destroyed in the French Revolution, but later restored by Louis-Philippe who reigned from 1830 to 1848.

Miss Moberly and Miss Jourdain spent much of the day touring the palace itself, then rested in the *Galerie des Glaces*, a spectacular Hall of Mirrors.

About four in the afternoon, Miss Moberly suggested they should visit the Petit Trianon. The Petit Trianon is one of the smaller palaces at Versailles. It's a columned building, set in vast gardens, that was designed in the reign of Louis XV. But its most famous resident was Queen Marie Antoinette, who was given the house by her husband, Louis XVI in 1774.

To reach the Petit Trianon, you walk about a 1½ km (1 mile) north-west of the main palace. The two ladies consulted their guide map and set off, but quickly lost their way. They ended up on a narrow lane at right angles to the main drive. They walked north for a bit and circled several buildings, then realised they were lost and asked directions from two men they took to be gardeners. Unfortunately, they got confused and lost their way again. After passing the *Temple de L'Amour* (Temple of Love) one of the area's minor attractions, Miss Moberly started to feel ... peculiar. Although she had thoroughly enjoyed the visit so far, she was suddenly seized by a black depression which she could not seem to shake off. Recalling the feeling later, she claimed there was absolutely no cause for it. She wasn't tired and she was very interested in the buildings around her. Not wanting to spoil things, she said nothing. What she didn't realise until much later, was that Miss Jourdain was feeling peculiar too. For her, the whole area had taken on an aura of loneliness and depression. She had the unpleasant sensation that she was walking in her sleep. But like Miss Moberly, she said nothing either. Things started to get stranger.

They met up with a number of people in the gardens of the Petit Trianon ... all of them wearing very old-fashioned clothing. When they spoke, they used an old form of French. The two ladies emerged eventually into the front drive and the feeling of oppression suddenly lifted. Without discussing what had happened, they took a carriage to their hotel and had a very welcome cup of tea.

For a week, neither woman said anything about her experience. Then they began to compare notes. They agreed about the people in historical costume speaking an old-fashioned form of French, but one woman Miss Moberly had seen was not noticed at all by Miss Jourdain even though (as far as Miss Moberly was concerned) they had both walked right up to her. Faced with this mystery, they agreed each should write down a full, detailed account of her experience after which they could investigate the matter properly. This they did, but it was fully three years before they returned to Versailles and again visited the Petit Trianon.

What they found was astonishing. The place was nothing like the Petit Trianon they'd seen before. At first they thought it had all been modernised, but when they made inquiries they discovered no building work or renovations had taken place since their last visit. They took to their history books and quickly found pictures of the Trianon they'd seen, the Trianon not as it was now, but as it had been at the time of Louis XVI. A woman they'd met briefly looked exactly like the old portraits of Marie Antoinette (Louis XVI's wife).

A few years later, Misses Moberly and Jourdain found the courage to publish a full, detailed account of their experience. (They called it *An Adventure*.) The book was an immediate sensation, but some time after its publication, critics discovered a fancy dress party had been held in the Trianon by a friend of the distinguished writer Marcel Proust. Everybody assumed the two ladies had stumbled into the party and mistaken play-action for reality. Their publisher decided this made sense and allowed their book to go out of print. But it later turned out this explanation wouldn't do. The fancy dress party was held in 1894 – seven years before Miss Moberly and Miss

Jourdain visited the Trianon.

There's still no logical explanation for what happened to them and the case of the 'ghosts of Versailles' as it's often called remains a favourite topic for speculation among psychical researchers (people who study the paranormal). But one thing seems certain – this is no ordinary 'ghost' story. Spirits of the dead may still haunt the Palace of Versailles, but that's not what the Misses Moberly and Jourdain saw. What they saw was the entire place – buildings, gardens, people – as it was in the days of Louis XVI. And that means they stepped back in time.

Chapter 4

The Man Who Witnessed History

The Misses Moberly and Jourdain only stepped back in time once – so far as we know, nothing like it ever happened to them again. But a distinguished, scholar made something of a habit of it.

Ten years after the Versailles adventure, a young British academic named Arnold Toynbee experienced something like a time-quake when he found himself transported from Oxford to a back yard in the Roman town of Teanum in 80 BC. There he watched horrified as a leader of the Italian Confederacy committed suicide after being betrayed by his wife (the Italian confederacy was a collection of states that opposed the power of

Rome). Then Toynbee snapped back abruptly to the present day. At the time, he thought he'd had a peculiar vision triggered by reading of the incident.

But then it happened again. A year later, in 1912, Toynbee took himself off to Greece with the intention of visiting a few of the many historical sites in that country. One that attracted him particularly was the scene of an ancient and important battle. As Toynbee sat on a highland peak at Pharsalus, staring down across the sunlit countryside, his mind turned to the 2nd century BC when the Roman legions commanded by Titus Quinctius Flamininus faced the army of Philip V of Macedon. It was part of a conflict that had been grumbling on for years. Rome sought to extend its power across the Adriatic. Philip tried to stop them but found himself on the losing side and was forced to make peace in 205 BC. But the Romans still saw

him as a thorn in their side and just five years later they decided to settle things once and for all.

As young Toynbee considered these matters, he suddenly 'slipped into a time pocket' (the words are his own) and found the world around him had changed. The most noticeable difference was the weather. In place of the bright sunshine, he was surrounded by a mist so thick and gloomy that he could scarcely make out the contours of the land below.

For a moment he sat bewildered by what was happening to him, then the mist parted and he found himself witness to a battle fought more than 1,000 years before. The Macedonian forces held the high ground. The Roman legions were ranged below. Philip saw his opportunity and charged, but Flamininus spotted a weakness in the Macedonian flank.

With all the ruthlessness that characterised Ancient Rome, he wheeled his men and attacked with such relentless fury that a sickened Toynbee had to turn his face away. It was the end of the battle and, politically, the end for Philip, who was permitted to remain King of Macedon, but only as a prisoner in his own country, firmly under the Roman thumb.

Toynbee blinked and the horror of the ancient war vanished. He was back on his hill, looking down on the peaceful, sunlit scene. The experience was as weird as those of Jane O'Neill and the Misses Moberly and Jourdain, but weirder still was to come – and soon. A couple of months later, Toynbee had left Greece for Crete. On March 19th he was mountain walking when he stumbled on a ruined villa of the type built by the Venetian governors of the island three centuries earlier.

He was doing no more than looking at the ruins when something hit him. He later described the experience as 'like the deep drop of an aeroplane when it falls into an air pocket.' Instantly he was back 250 years in time to the day the house was evacuated. Toynbee watched the events for a few minutes, then returned to his own time as abruptly as he left.

Before long he was to experience a third, and far more spectacular time slip. His travels took him to Turkey and the Biblical city of Ephesus. While visiting the empty ruins of the open-air amphitheatre there, he suddenly found himself surrounded by a throng of people ... all of whom had been dead for almost 1,900 years. Toynbee realised at once what he was watching: an event described dramatically in Acts 19 of the New Testament in the Bible, when St Paul the Apostle and two of his companions had a confrontation with the silversmiths' guild.

The problem was that Paul had not confined himself to preaching Christianity in what was then a pagan city, but had also encouraged anyone who'd listen not to buy silver images of the goddess Diana who was worshipped in the local temple. For the silversmiths, this was clearly bad for business. One of them, a man named Demetrius, loudly bemoaned: '...not only is our

craft in danger...but also the temple of the great goddess Diana, worshipped throughout Asia and the world, will be despised, and her magnificence ... destroyed.' An indignant crowd gathered in the theatre and hurled abuse at the Christians for nearly two hours before an official finally persuaded them to go home. Even then they left chanting grumpily, 'Great is Diana of the Ephesians!'

All of it was witnessed by Toynbee, who was able to pick out Paul's two companions Gaius and Aristarchus and even recognize a Jew named Alexander who tried to help. Then, as the chant died away, he emerged from this latest time pocket into the present day.

But a month later, he was back in another one. By now returned to Greece, he was visiting the ancient coastal town of Monemvasia in the Laconia region. Monemvasia lies at the foot of a massive offshore rock that is overlooked by the ruins of a medieval fortress and a 14th century Byzantine church. It was the fortress that interested him. The great keep had been a refuge for the Greeks during invasions

by neighbouring states and became one of the most important commercial centres in the Middle Ages. Now, however, it was falling to ruins. Toynbee found a gap in the ancient walls and climbed through. His attention was drawn to the remnants of several bronze cannons half covered by undergrowth.

At once he was back in 1715, witnessing the violent result of a Turkish takeover. Until that time, the fortress had been in Venetian hands, but was granted to the Turks in a peaceful settlement. Once the Turks took control, however, they breached the walls and toppled the cannons so the fort would never again become a danger to them.

Less than a month later, Toynbee was to experience his most significant time slip. It was related to the Franks who established the most powerful Christian kingdom of early medieval western Europe and subsequently gave their name to France. During the early 13th century, the Franks built a new fortress city, Mistra, southwest of Sparta in the same region of Greece as the Monemvasia fortress. It flourished for about two

centuries before falling into a gradual decline until it was overrun and ruined during the Greek War of Independence which raged from 1821 to 1832. Toynbee wanted to see it.

May 1912 found him sitting in the ruined citadel of Mistra, staring out across the Plain of Sparta and munching on a bar of chocolate. Then came the now-familiar sensation of falling into an air pocket and suddenly he was watching the massacre that left the city in ruins. What made this experience different to the others was the effect it had on him. He was struck by 'a horrifying sense of the sin manifest in the conduct of human affairs' and decided this was something he had to write about. The result, in 1934, was the first book of what was to become a monumental 12-volume masterwork entitled *A Study of History*. You can read his personal account of the time slips in Volume 10.

Chapter 5

The Man Who Visited a Roman Orgy

Arnold Toynbee was at least thinking about the past when he had his experiences of time slip. Malcolm Turner was thinking about burglars. In 1986, Turner and his wife Evelyn were on their way from their Surrey home to spend a weekend with friends in Kent when they remembered they'd left behind some gifts they'd intended to bring with them. They turned the car and headed back.

Mr Turner was a successful businessman running his own company. His home was impressive, with a large yard, outbuildings and stables. He headed for those stables now, since that's where they had left the box of gifts. There were lights in one of the outbuildings.

The couple looked at one another. Evelyn Turner had a horror of fire and they always switched off the power before they left home, so it wasn't a question of leaving the lights on accidentally. This almost certainly had to be burglars.

Malcolm Turner found something he could use as a club and climbed out of the car. He told his wife he was going to investigate, but in the meantime he wanted her to turn the car and, if it did prove to be intruders, drive quickly to a neighbour's home and phone the police. Then he walked towards the lighted building.

Afterwards he confessed that part of him was convinced the sound of the car would probably have frightened off any burglars, but as he got closer he heard music coming from inside, along with raised voices. In a moment of extraordinary courage, he flung open the door.

What he found was not what he expected, not anything he *could* have expected. The inside of the building was brightly lit, but full of smoke and haze

so that everything was a complete blur. He strained to see what was going on – he suspected drug-users might have taken over the place for a party – but in vain. Then, abruptly, everything snapped into focus.

Malcolm Turner found himself standing inside a large wooden building with steam issuing from an enclosure at the far end. The place was lit by torches and there was a large fire in the middle. He was not the only one there. The overheated chamber was jam-packed with men and women in various stages of undress, most of them drinking heavily.

He looked around, scarcely able to believe his eyes, and took in more details. The walls had been painted in bright, stark colours. There were cauldrons of hot food. Strangest of all, there were several racks of ancient weapons.

Turner swung his gaze back to the throng of people. While many of them were completely naked, a few were still fully dressed ... in fitted breastplates. It was incredible, but this modern-day businessman had walked back in time and into the middle of a Roman orgy.

Since everyone seemed far too busy to pay any attention to him, he went on a tour of inspection. He looked closely at the racked swords, the jugs of wine, the massive cooking pots. There was an overpowering smell of spices and the noise from the revellers was almost deafening. He tried to engage one of the Romans in conversation, but the man ignored him. The same thing happened again and again.

Turner tried to touch someone and his hand went right through the man's shoulder. Yet there was nothing ghostly about the scene. Sounds, sights, smells, even the taste in the back of his throat were as vivid as anyone could expect, yet he quickly discovered nothing could be touched. It was as if the orgy was real enough, but Turner himself was the ghost.

He walked to the far end of the room and found a raised podium draped in an enormous flag. High above was the battle standard and imperial eagle of the Roman legions.

A feeling of unease began to creep over Turner. His earlier curiosity was slowly replaced by a nagging worry. Suppose he was stuck here and couldn't get back? Suppose he was condemned to haunt this ancient party forever? He started to shiver and made his way quickly back to the part of the building where he had entered.

There was no longer any door. The area was gloomy, almost dark. The wooden walls that made up the remainder of the building had been replaced by a sheet of something looking curiously like steel. Before it, a group of soldiers squatted playing dice.

One of the men made a bad throw, seized the dice cup and hurled it in Turner's direction. Another got up and went to retrieve it. As the second man approached, he stopped suddenly, only 30 centimetres or so away. His face took on an expression of amazement, then fear. He started to shout to the others. Clearly Turner had now become visible to the others in the room.

The soldiers began to rush towards him. He stepped back and realised that his surroundings had become solid – he could touch things for the first time. He caught his heel on an object on the floor, toppled backwards and crashed against the wall ... to find himself outside the outbuilding in his own time again.

As far as he was concerned, Malcolm Turner spent several minutes in the Roman past, but his wife experienced the incident rather differently.

Still seated in their car, ready to drive off at a moment's notice, she watched her husband walk determinedly to the outbuilding and fling open the door. She saw the sudden glare of light, heard noise and watched him step inside. The door bounced back closed of its own accord, then opened again almost immediately. There was Malcolm walking out again, silhouetted against the glare.

Evelyn flung open the car door and rushed towards him. As she did so the light behind him slowly faded, as did the sound of voices and, more slowly still, curious aromas of perfumes and cooking. Suddenly they were both standing in the rain looking into their empty and unlit building.

Chapter 6

A Trip to Medieval Times

Many, perhaps most, time slips occur to people on their own. A few, like the Versailles adventure, involve two people. The weirdness that occurred on a cold October weekend in 1957 managed to suck in three.

On the weekend in question, a class of teenage cadets with HMS *Ganges,* a Royal Navy shore training establishment at Shotley, in Suffolk, was sent off on a survival exercise. Nobody was told where they were going, but the 20-strong group left the *Ganges* early on the Saturday afternoon and travelled for two or three hours towards Ipswich until, after negotiating various country roads and lanes they arrived at a farmyard where they were billeted overnight in a barn.

The following morning was frosty, but bright and

sunny. Class trainers decided to split the boys into groups. One group, consisting of 15-year-old cadets William Lang, Michael Crowley and Ray Baker, was given the assignment of finding a village named Kersey, then returning to report back on everything they saw.

They followed a road for a time, then cut across some fields. Here came the first faint hint of the strangeness to come. Bill Lang stumbled on a hare, but instead of running off, the animal simply lay there looking at him. He actually picked it up and while it seemed completely uninjured, the hare made no attempt to struggle. He set it down again and it loped off.

Shortly afterwards, the boys came across a grey stone cottage surrounded by large oak trees. A farm labourer was standing with his wife and family, leaning on the gate. For some reason he seemed suspicious of the cadets and made no attempt to greet them until they asked him how to get to Kersey. Even then he only pointed and said shortly, 'Hold in that direction.'

Only 10 minutes later, they came in sight of the

village. From their vantage point, they could see the roofs of the houses and the high tower of Kersey Church. They also clearly heard the sound of church bells as they left the fields to take the laneway down into the village. But as they approached within 100 metres of the church itself, the bells abruptly stopped.

If you ever have the pleasure of visiting Kersey today, you'll find yourself in a wholly charming English village. You can see the church tower for miles and the church itself – first built in Saxon times, then rebuilt by the Normans – is visible from just about everywhere in the village.

There's a well-made tarmacadam road running through Kersey and its picturesque stream – called the Water-Splash – is spanned in the eastern quarter by an ornamental footbridge. Several of the houses have been painted pink and, like so many English villages, many nestle in well-kept gardens. There is a scattering of thatched cottages, a couple of pleasant pubs – The Bell and The White Horse – a pottery, a restaurant, a general store and a little post office.

All in all, you can easily see how it earned its reputation as (in the words of one official source) 'the most picturesque village of South Suffolk.' But the village you see today is a far cry from the Kersey visited by the three cadets.

The first thing of note was that the church, which had been visible from the fields above the village, was now hidden behind trees growing on the mound on which the building stands. With the church bells stopped, the boys walked in an eerie silence until, turning a corner, they had their first sight of the village itself.

The stream was still there, running down the centre of the village, but the tarmacadam road was gone, as were most of the houses. In their place was a dirt track with two or three miserable-looking dwellings widely scattered on its left hand side. There were no houses or cottages at all on the right, just tall forest trees.

The track ran down to the stream, then rose beyond it to the northern end of the village where there were a few more houses, all of them dirty, small and old. The stream was crossed by a bridge,

but nothing like the bridge that's there today: it was no more than two wooden planks with four posts and a handrail.

Eternal Recurrence

The Russian philosopher P. D. Ouspensky came up with an idea of a type of time travel very different to that experienced by the people mentioned in the last few chapters. In a weird novel called The Strange Life of Ivan Osokin, *he examined the terrifying theme of eternal recurrence. This is the way he thought eternal occurrence might work:*

You are born, let's say, in 1992. You live a perfectly normal life until you die of old age in 2080. But at the exact instant of your death, you are born again in 1992 and proceed to live the same life again until your death in 2080 … at which point you are born again in 1992.

Ouspensky allowed his fictional hero to exercise free will during each loop of the eternal recurrence, but in his more serious,

non-fiction works he was much less optimistic. He thought we are all doomed to repeat exactly the same thoughts, actions and mistakes forever.

There were no people about at all. The only living things they could see were some motionless ducks on the waters of the stream. Perhaps stranger still, there were no parked cars, no telephone lines, no TV or radio aerials – nothing at all, in fact, to suggest a modern lifestyle. The silence was complete. There wasn't even a hint of birdsong.

The boys went down to the stream and scooped out some water to drink. They felt, they admitted later, uneasy and depressed, similar sensations to those experienced by the Misses Moberly and Jourdain on their time trip to Versailles. There was another similarity as well. When, years later, William Lang was told that Miss Moberly had described the trees at Versailles as 'flat and lifeless like a wood worked in tapestry,' he confirmed that this was how he had experienced the trees at Kersey. The whole place had a horribly unpleasant feel about it, without wind, sounds or even shadows.

But the flat and lifeless look wasn't the only problem with the trees. They were green with spring buds. Yet this was October – well into autumn. Both village pubs and all but one of Kersey's shops had disappeared. The boys jumped the stream and went to examine the one shop remaining, a butcher's in which skinned ox carcasses were hanging. But the meat was literally green with age and the whole place covered in filthy cobwebs as if it had been left derelict for months. Other buildings were equally strange. Not one seemed to have furniture, or even curtains.

The boys had the eerie feeling of being watched, although there was not so much as a dog on the street, and their unease increased. Their slow progress up the village street got faster and faster until suddenly they were running for their lives. They turned a corner at the top of the street and stopped, breathless, to look back...

The church bells chimed, the church itself was clearly visible, the village was repopulated. Normality had returned. This case-study, one of the strangest in modern times, was thoroughly investigated in the late 1980s by the Vice President of the Society for Psychical Research, Andrew MacKenzie. He concluded that the three boys had somehow travelled back to medieval times when Kersey was hurriedly abandoned after an outbreak of the Black Death.

Chapter 7

An Attack from the Past

After the success of his first book, the writer John Jefferies took six months leave from his day job and rented a large cottage in the west of Scotland so he could work in peace and quiet on his new novel. The place seemed ideal when John and his wife Stella moved in. They hired a woman from the nearby village to cook and clean for them, began to make friends in the locality and got down to work. But then the strangeness started.

The first hint of anything amiss came when they discovered their cook would not, under any circumstances, prepare a late evening meal. In fact she refused, point-blank, to work in the house at all after dark.

Then they decided to hold a dinner party and sent out invitations to their new friends in the village.

One after another, the refusals came in. Previous appointment ... unable to attend ... much regret ... until, to their astonishment, they found not a single person was willing to come.

It was Stella Jefferies who discovered what was wrong. She was shopping in a nearby town when she struck up a conversation with another woman who remarked that the local bay had a reputation for being haunted. Then the woman realised Stella was renting the cottage overlooking the bay and refused to say anything more.

All the same, the move turned out to be a huge success. John finished his new book. Stella sold a series of articles about the plants and wildlife of the district. John's book proved extremely successful and Stella was asked to work on a TV wildlife series. Everything was going very well indeed. In fact the only small cloud on the horizon was that their stay in Scotland was almost over. The lease on their cottage had almost run out and the time of their return to London was almost upon them. They decided to turn their final three weeks into a holiday.

For several days they became tourists, visiting the local sights, but then as sometimes happens in Scotland, it began to rain heavily and wouldn't stop, so they spent a day at home. By afternoon, John was struggling with his crossword while Stella was correcting proofs. Both were surprised to hear a pistol shot outside.

Sailors sometimes shoot off pistols as signals when their boats get into trouble and John suspected something of this sort must have happened so he raced outside at once. To his absolute astonishment, there was a huge sailing ship in the bay. The noise he'd heard was not a pistol shot at all, but the snap of its sails in the wind.

The ship itself was a fascinating sight, built like the great galleons that sailed the seas in the 16th century. Sailors in old-fashioned costume swarmed over the rigging and some members of the crew struggled to launch a boat. John only realised they were all working in bright sunshine after a few moments.

He turned to call to Stella and at once discovered

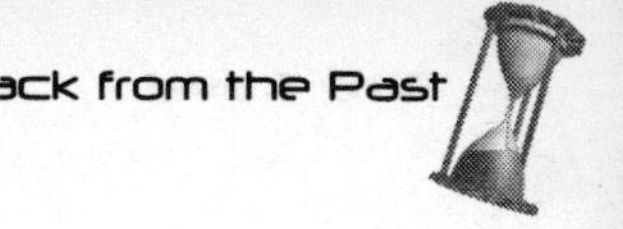

something creepy. Behind him it was still raining heavily. In fact, black rain clouds filled the whole sweep of the sky, except for a circle about 300 metres in diameter bathed in brilliant sunshine. The ship was at its centre.

Stella came out to join him and at once noticed something else weird. The wind that was filling the ship's sails was blowing in the opposite direction to the movement of the clouds and the trees on the other side of the bay. This was so odd as to be almost impossible and she more than half decided her eyes must be playing tricks. She ran back indoors for binoculars.

John watched with growing fear as the longboat launched from the ship drew closer to the shore. He told himself that there had to be a logical explanation for what was happening, but all his instincts warned him this was trouble – and big trouble at that. Stella came out of the house and handed him the binoculars. 'That's a Spanish warship,' she told him.

John raised the binoculars from his eyes and found he didn't doubt her for a moment. Crazy though it seemed, they both knew they were watching a ship of the Spanish Armada, presumably fleeing from the battle with Drake's fleet in the great turning-point of British history during the reign of Queen Elizabeth I. Through the binoculars, John could see the damage to the structure made by British guns and the hasty repairs carried out by the Spanish crew.

The longboat filled with enemy sailors drew closer to the shore. 'Shall we make a run for it?' John asked. His wife shook her head. It was best to keep still, she thought. Probably they hadn't been noticed by the men below and moving would only draw attention to themselves.

So they stood still as the boat beached. Sailors climbed out less than 50 metres away, unloading water casks. Their officer was a young man in his early twenties, armed with a pistol and clearly very nervous. Suddenly he caught sight of them and swung the pistol in their direction.

For an instant, it seemed he would shoot, but then he shouted something and pointed at the water casks. John realised at once the ship was short of drinking water and pointed towards a well in a nearby garden. The men promptly ran towards it and began to fill their casks.

Everything was happening at breakneck speed now. As each cask was filled, the men rolled it down the slope and loaded it onto their longboat. When they were finished, the young officer turned back towards John and Stella. There was a tense

moment during which they wondered again if he was going to shoot them, but instead he doffed his hat with a flourish, bowed briefly then jumped into the boat.

The longboat reached the ship and the supplies of water were winched aboard. John could see bandaged sailors make their way painfully on crutches across the deck desperate for a drink. Then the longboat itself was hoisted back on board and the galleon started to make its way out to sea.

Then, like the throwing of a light switch, the great sailing ship simply vanished; and with it went the wide circle of sunlight. John and Stella were standing in the pouring rain, shocked, frightened and bewildered, desperately trying to come to terms with what they'd just seen and, naturally, wondering if it could possibly have been real.

Only metres away on the beach, the sailors' footprints were still visible, as were the furrows made in the sand as the barrels were rolled along and the deep gouge made by the longboat as it beached. But only for a while. In moments the heavy downpour had washed them all away.

Chapter 8

It Could Happen to You

Occasionally, time slip can be experienced by some members of a party, but not others. A case in point concerns the American biologist Ivan Sanderson who travelled with his wife and their professional assistant, Fred Allsop, to Haiti to conduct a biological survey.

The three of them were engaged in field research in an isolated area of the island when their car got stuck in the mud and they had to walk home. Fred Allsop was in the lead and eventually moved some distance ahead. Sanderson and his wife were walking together. All of a sudden their environment changed. One minute they were walking through desolate countryside, the next they found themselves surrounded by houses. Sanderson described them like this:[2]

[2] In *'Things' and More 'Things'* Pyramid Books, New York, 1967.

> *These houses hung out over the road, which suddenly appeared to be muddy with large cobblestones. The houses were of (I would say) about the Elizabethan period of England, but for some reason I knew they were in Paris. They had pent roofs, with some dormer windows, gables, timbered porticoes and small windows with tiny leaded panes. Here and there, there were dull reddish lights burning behind them, as if from candles. There were iron frame lanterns hanging from timbers jutting from some houses and they were all swaying together as if in a wind, but there was not the faintest movement of the air about us.*

Sanderson's wife stopped dead and he walked into her. Unable to trust his own eyes, Sanderson asked, 'What's wrong?' She stared around her, wide-eyed, then took his hand and whispered, 'How did we get to Paris 500 years ago?'

Still unable to believe what was happening, Sanderson asked her to describe what she saw. It was night, but the whole scene was lit by bright moonlight. They compared detail after detail and pointed out various aspects of the houses to one another. It was obvious they were both seeing exactly the same thing.

After a while a feeling of weakness overcame them and they started to sway. Sanderson called to Fred – he could still see his white shirt in the distance – then collapsed in a fit of dizziness onto a kerbstone. Fred ran back but by the time he reached them, the houses had disappeared. He told them he'd seen nothing at all unusual at any point of their walk. Although no longer evident on the island today, Parisian-style houses are very much a part of Haiti's past. The French colonised the island in 1697.

What happened to the Sandersons was typical of almost all time-slip experiences in that it happened quite unexpectedly. They weren't thinking about time, they weren't talking about time and their attention wasn't focused on the past. All either of them wanted was to get home and get to bed.

The author Stephen Jenkins wasn't thinking about the past either. He was out for a country walk near Mounts Bay in Cornwall when he saw a large group of armed men in period costume crouching in the bushes beside the track up ahead. With a lot more courage than I'd have shown, he ran shouting towards them. Then there was a sensation like passing through a curtain of warm air and suddenly the men were no longer there.

Villainous bands of armed men are very much a part of Cornwall's piratical past. It's possible, if you believe in such things[3], that Mr Jenkins was seeing

[3] As I do. See my *Ghosthunter's Handbook* published by Faber and Faber, 2004.

ghosts, but the curtain sensation suggests that in running towards them he moved from one time stratum to another – a typical time slip experience. Except that there really is no *typical* time-slip experience. They can happen to anybody – even you – anywhere, at any time, without the slightest warning. Sometimes they can happen without your even noticing.

A man named P. J. Chase of Wallington in Surrey was waiting for a bus one afternoon in 1968 when he decided to stroll a little way down the road to pass the time. He came across two very nice little thatched cottages with hollyhocks in their gardens, one of them dated to 1837, according to a plaque on its wall. Mr Chase admired the cottages for a while, then strolled back and caught his bus.

It wasn't until the following day he discovered he'd walked into another time-stream. He happened to mention the cottages to a friend, who looked puzzled and told him that while she knew the area very well, she'd never seen the cottages he described.

Intrigued, the two of them went to check and found the friend was right. The only buildings at the spot were two brick houses. But a local resident confirmed that the cottages *had* existed at one time. They'd been pulled down to make room for the houses some years previously.

Chapter 9

The Illusion of Time

What's happening here? The eight chapters you've just read are not fiction – they're fact – and well-investigated fact at that.

- Jane O'Neill's visit to Fotheringhay Church was investigated by the distinguished author Colin Wilson.
- Misses Moberly and Jourdain published an extensive firsthand account of their Versailles adventure, as did Arnold Toynbee on his experiences in Greece.
- The reports of Malcolm Turner's Roman orgy and John and Stella Jefferies' encounter with the Spanish sailors were collected by the respected British journalist Colin Parsons.

- Paranormal investigator Andrew MacKenzie interviewed all three of the former Cadets who wandered briefly into the Middle Ages.
- Ivan Sanderson is a respected scientist and a trained observer. He joins a lengthy list of individuals who have nothing to gain except ridicule by publishing accounts of their time slip experiences.

Yet the accounts themselves make no sense. They contradict everything you know about time. For example, you probably think of time as a river, something with a beginning and an end that flows from the past to the future, sweeping you – and everything else – along with it. We sail on time's river and once objects and actions fall into the past, they are lost and gone forever. They don't exist any more, so the idea of somehow 'going back' to visit them is a nonsense.

That's certainly how you experience time, but it's not necessarily how time really is. Let's begin with the idea of time moving in a line, starting *here* and heading *there* – time's arrow as philosophers like to call it. This is linear time.

I know it's hard to believe, but many of what you think of as your own ideas are actually picked up without even noticing from the people around you. Judaism, Islam and Christianity all emphasise a straight-line vision of time (beginning with a creation and ending in an apocalypse or judgement) which means most people in the Western world tend to think that way as well.

The idea of linear time is even framed in verse. When the great Persian poet Omar Khayyam wrote his frequently quoted lines: The moving finger writes, and having writ moves on, *he was describing the common vision of time as a process which generates a past beyond our power to reach or change.*

If you're one of them, it can come as a bit of a shock to discover not everybody shares your

certainties. There are several other beliefs – notably Hinduism, Buddhism and Jainism – that see time as circular. They see a Great Wheel of Time revolving within eternity allowing individuals and civilisations to appear and disappear, incarnating and reincarnating, until, at the end of each cycle, the world itself is destroyed ... only to be born again.

That's a very old idea. It was accepted by every ancient culture, East and West, with the sole exceptions of the Hebrews and the Persians. The Stoics of Ancient Greece thought the whole process was linked to the stars and taught that when the planets and constellations returned to their original positions, the universe would be renewed.

And funnily enough, it's an idea that has scientific backing. As long ago as the 19th century the physicist Henri Poincaré produced a theorem showing that, given enough time, any closed system will return to the state it was in when it began. If you have an unlimited amount of time, then the system will return to its beginnings again and again, forever.

Bishop Nemesius of Emesa, who lived in the 4th century, had a somewhat similar idea to Poincaré when he announced that: '... each individual man will live again, with the same friends and fellow citizens. They will go through the same experiences and the same activities. Every city, village and field will be restored, just as it was. And this restoration of the universe takes place not once, but over and over again – indeed to all eternity without end.'

Since our universe is a closed system, Poincaré's Return – as the theorem is called – supports the Stoics and the Hindus. The universe will eventually end by getting back where it started then repeating itself again and again. But when you think about it, that doesn't help much with our case histories. Because whether it runs straight or in a circle, everybody still thinks of time moving in *one direction*, from this minute to the next minute, then the one after that.

If time flies like an arrow, common sense and personal experience both tell you it's *impossible* to get back from this minute to the last. But while circular time allows that you will get back to the last minute eventually, if you want to get there *now*, you have to jump instantly forward to the end of the universe and beyond which common sense and personal experience both tell you isn't very likely to happen either. The question is, can you trust common sense and personal experience?

Common sense and experience will tell you the world is flat. I know you *know* it isn't, but that's because you've seen the satellite photos or worked it out from watching ships sink below the horizon. What you *experience* is a flat world. Common sense and experience will tell you the Sun goes round the Earth. You can see it happening any day. But what you see isn't what you get. The apparent movement of the Sun is an illusion caused by the rotation of the Earth. An awful lot of first-class scientists have been telling us for centuries that what you experience as time is an illusion as well.

Chapter 10

Newtonian Time

The rot set in during the 17th century, although nobody really noticed then. It was started by Sir Isaac Newton, a man your teachers will probably tell you was the Father of Physics, without necessarily mentioning he was a magician, astrologer, alchemist (tried to turn base metal into gold) and lunatic as well.

The magical interests are well documented. The lunacy showed up in episodes of madness throughout his life. He couldn't control his temper and once threatened to burn both his step-parents alive, then torch their house. But despite (or possibly because of) all this he was a towering genius. His calculations laid the foundations of modern physics and the laws he discovered are still used by engineers to this day.

Newton thought of time exactly the way you do. He's on record as saying that, 'Absolute, true and mathematical time of itself and from its own nature flows equably and without relation to anything external.' Note the word 'flows'. Newton saw time like a river, moving from here to there in a strictly one-way trip. He also saw time as an absolute, a thing in itself stitched into the very fabric of nature and beyond any possibility of influence. He was confident that if one of the clocks he liked making showed it was midnight in Woolsthorpe[4], then it would also be midnight (or at least its local equivalent) on Epsilon Aurigae and everywhere else in the universe. But that was because he never took the trouble to think through the implications of his own mathematics.

[4] The place he was born.

You've probably already learned Newton's famous Three Laws of Motion. The first states that if anything solid is sitting still or moving in a straight line at a constant speed, it'll stay that way forever unless some force acts on it. The third states that for any action you get an equal and opposite reaction.

The second law is a bit more tricky. It states that 'the time rate of change of the velocity or acceleration of a body is directly proportional to the force applied and inversely proportional to the mass m of the body.' In other words, the harder you push it the faster it goes, but a big object will move slower than a small one. Of course Newton didn't just express his laws in words, he worked out the mathematics as well.

There are only three kinds of people in the world – those who understand mathematics and those who don't. I'm very much in the latter category, so I'll keep this simple. You really only need to know two things. The first is that if you multiply a negative number by another negative number, the result is always positive (e.g. –2 x –2 = +4 and not -4).

The second is that in the mathematical calculation of Newton's second law, the value for time is *squared.* To square something you multiply it by itself, so 2 squared is 2 x 2, 3 squared is 3 x 3 and so on. For time squared, you take whatever value of time you're looking at (say 3 years) and multiply it by itself: 3 years x 3 years.

Now take a deep breath, because what comes next is astonishing. Time running forwards in the familiar way is expressed by ordinary numbers in Newton's maths. But time running backwards (which I know you think is nonsense, but bear with me) is shown by using negative numbers, expressed with a minus sign before them. So if you wanted to talk about three years of *backwards* time, you would write it as –3.

Newton didn't actually consider negative time very much. He simply calculated the formulae needed to make things work in the normal world. But those formulae let you see how things really are and if you change ordinary time to negative time in Newton's second law, it makes no difference to the outcome. It's impossible, but what Newton

figured out without even realising it was that the world still works perfectly well if time starts running backwards.

Why does it still work properly? Because time in the formula is squared. It's multiplied by itself. Negative time multiplied by itself always gives you positive time, so the equation reverts back to what it was and everything continues to behave exactly the way it always did.

You may think of your life as starting with your birth and ending with your death. But it's just as reasonable to think of it as starting with you rising from your grave and ending when you're sucked into your mother's womb. In other words, reversing the direction of time doesn't run contrary to the laws of Newton's physics – which is very good news if you're interested in time travel. The only problem is that while time *could* run backwards if it wanted, it never really seems to. How many people do you know who are living their lives backwards? ... No, me neither.

Perhaps more to the point, we're both surrounded by things that only ever happen one

way. You can't unscramble an egg. You can't pour milk out of your tea. You've probably dropped a dozen plates and watched them smash to pieces on the ground... but you've never, ever, watched those pieces join themselves together and jump back into your hand.

None of this may worry you, but it's exactly the sort of thing that causes scientists to lose sleep. Newton's laws really work. We use them to build aeroplanes and send spaceships to Mars. So you have to figure out why, when it comes to things like scrambling an egg, nature always seems to contradict them. (You're probably so used to scrambling eggs, you never think of the process as contradicting the laws of physics, but according to Newton you should notice the egg unscrambling itself anything up to 50% of the time.)

There has to be an explanation for this and scientists have gone batty for years trying to find it. One notion they came up with was based on the idea that while there are about a billion ways to break a plate, there's only one way to put it back together again. Thus the plate that joins itself

together and jumps back into your hand isn't actually impossible, just terribly, terribly rare. So rare, in fact, that nobody in the whole history of plate breaking has ever seen it happening.

Another more sophisticated notion was that dissipated energy – the sound of the plate smashing, the small but real vibration of the floor and so on – complicated the picture so much that it created a one-way time flow without actually contradicting Newton. Both these theories – and a lot of others – have proven unsatisfactory. But there's one explanation that's still worth considering. This is the idea that time isn't part of the physical universe at all, but is really just the way your mind works to make sense of the things you experience. This is a very clever notion, based on good evidence.

Psychologists have long known that your mind organises input to suit itself. Take your eye, for example. If you examine one of those cutaway illustrations of the lens, the laws of optics[5] prove you see everything upside down. But since an upside-down world isn't much use to anybody,

[5]. Another of Newton's contributions to physics.

your mind quietly reverses the image so you seem to see everything the right way up.

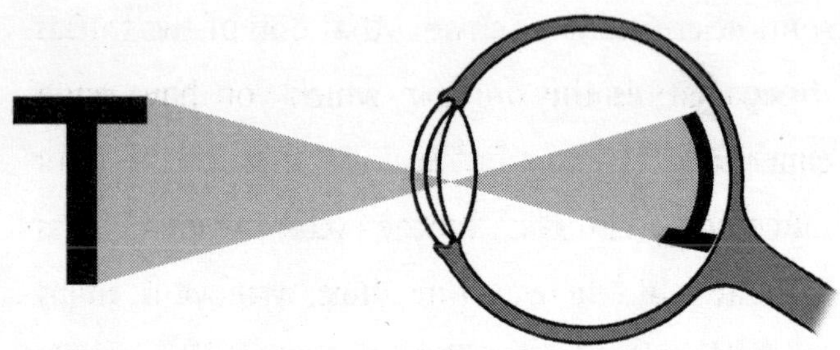

But it doesn't stop there. Your brain is peppered with all sorts of information every minute of the day. And what your mind does is to *organise* that information so it makes sense to you. It imposes *patterns* on the information that allow you to recognise what things are, so you always know when you're looking at a cat even though you've never seen *that particular* cat before.

You only realise the importance of all this when the mind loses its ability to organise, as happens in certain types of illness. One patient could see that a glove was some sort of container, but had no idea what to put into it. Another grabbed his wife's head and tried to put it on, having worked out logically that it had to be his hat. Once you know the way your mind organises information generally, it's a short enough step to proposing – as some scientists have done – that one of the things it organises is the *order* in which you have each experience.

According to this theory, your whole life is actually out there all at once, but your mind carefully picks its way through the various events step by step. Which means time is an illusion produced by the step-by-step approach. There were quite a few good reasons for thinking this theory might be at least partly true, but it has some tricky implications. One is that while your mind usually organises time as a one-way river, it should in theory be able to reorganise time in a different way. In other words, your mind should be capable of time travel.

Chapter 11

Dreaming of the Future

A small strangeness occurred in the life of John Dunne when he was 24. One night he dreamed that his watch had stopped at half past four and as he drifted awake, a crowd seemed to be chanting 'Look... look... look!' So he struck a match and looked. His watch, lying on the bedside table, really had stopped at half past four.

These were the days of mechanical watches. Dunne rewound his watch and went back to sleep. Next morning when he checked, he found the watch was still showing almost exactly the right time. Which meant he'd woken up at the precise moment it stopped... or possibly even a few minutes before.

Dreaming that your watch has stopped, then waking up to find it really *has* stopped that exact

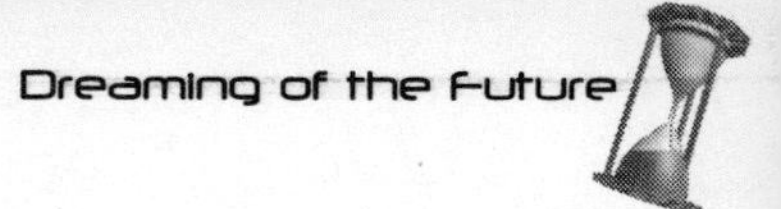

moment is pretty weird. But dreaming it's *about* to stop is a whole lot more spooky, because that means your mind has somehow travelled a little way through time into the future.

The problem with the watch incident was that there's no way to be sure what exactly happened. But two years later, in 1901, Dunne had another dream. He was in Italy at the time, having been invalided out of the Anglo-Boer War that was being fought in South Africa. But in his dream he found himself in Fashoda, in Egypt, a little way up the Nile from Khartoum.

The dream itself wasn't particularly vivid or in any way remarkable until three men appeared trekking up towards him from the south. All three were soldiers, dressed in ragged, faded khaki with their faces burned almost black by the sun. Dunne recognised them as members of his own column who had been marching in South Africa with him before he was wounded.

Even in the dream it seemed odd that they would have walked the length of the entire African continent as far as Egypt, but they assured him this was exactly what they had done. 'We've come right through from the Cape,' one said. Another added that he'd almost died from yellow fever.

Next morning, Dunne opened his copy of the *Daily Telegraph* and was stunned to see a headline that confirmed his dream: THE CAPE TO CAIRO: EXPEDITION AT KHARTOUM.

A year or so later, Dunne did it again. By now fully recovered from his war wound, he was back in South Africa and camping with the 6th Mounted Infantry in what was then the Orange Free State. This time the whole dream was unusually vivid. In it he found himself standing on high ground, like the spur of a hill or mountain. He knew at once that he

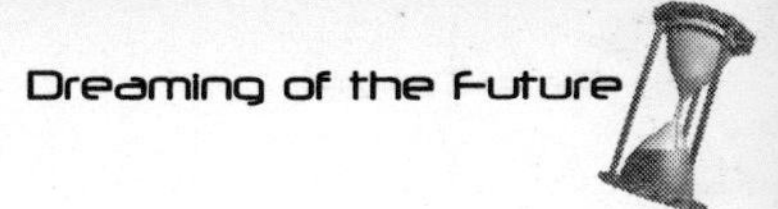

was on an island which was in imminent danger from a volcano. He then noticed there were jets of steam and smoke issuing from cracks in the ground. 'Good Lord!' he screamed. 'The whole thing is going to blow up!'

Experiments show that some people are capable of guessing the value of cards before *they are actually turned up. These experiments are usually quoted as examples of psychical talent, but they also have important implications where the possibility of time travel is concerned. If it is possible to foresee the future, even by a second or two, it means that the future is somehow there to be seen. Thus it is not time that flows like a river carrying us along from a disappearing past into a constantly created future. Rather it seems we are the ones who 'flow' examining events on our timeline as we go along.*

Immediately he was seized by the urgent necessity of evacuating the island – in the dream he somehow knew there were 4,000 inhabitants. The whole thing promptly turned into a nightmare. He was on a neighbouring island trying to persuade the French authorities there to send ships to save the people, but he kept being sent from one official to another as nobody would take responsibility for action. He actually woke up shouting, '4,000 people will be killed unless –'

With radio still in its early stage and the invention of television many years away, people found out what was going on in the world only through newspapers. But distribution was nothing like what it is today and the troops in South Africa received their papers in batches every few weeks.

In the next batch to arrive, Dunne opened the *Daily Telegraph* and saw the incredible headline:

VOLCANO DISASTER IN MARTINIQUE

TOWN SWEPT AWAY

AN AVALANCHE OF FLAME

PROBABLY LOSS OF OVER 40,000 LIVES

BRITISH STEAMER BURNT

Martinique, in the West Indies, was under French rule at the time and the explosion of the Mont Pelée volcano was one of the worst natural disasters for a century. But it quickly became clear that Dunne hadn't dreamed of the event in advance – he'd actually been dreaming about the newspaper headline. This was confirmed by the fact that he *misread* the seventh line and referred to the death toll as 4,000 (the figure in his dream) for 15 years afterwards.

John Dunne eventually left the army and became an aeronautics engineer. But he continued to monitor his dreams with interest and later attempted some serious experimental investigation. This led finally to the publication of his book *An Experiment with Time*, which caused a sensation when it was first published in 1927 and encouraged hundreds of people to experiment with their own dreams in the same way. Two unexpected discoveries arose.

One was prompted by a pair of predictive dreams Dunne had in 1904. In the first of these, he was standing on a bridge of planks with a single railing beyond which was a chasm filled with thick fog. Something emerged out of the fog and after a moment Dunne recognised it as a stream of water from a fire hose. As it played across the platform where he stood, he suddenly found himself surrounded by people. The fog turned to smoke, which rolled over everything, suffocating his companions.

In the evening paper next day, Dunne read a dramatic account of a fire in a French rubber

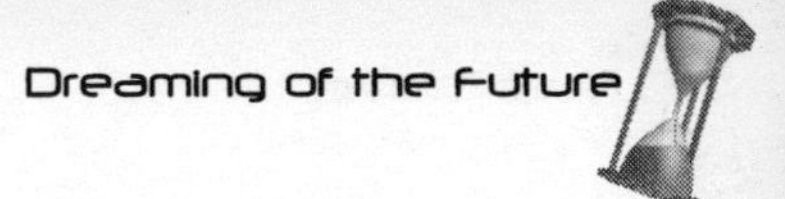

factory. Workers ran to safety on a balcony, which fire crews soaked in water to stop it catching alight. But their ladders were too short to reach the victims and while longer ladders were being fetched, thick black smoke rolled out of the building and suffocated everyone on the balcony.

Dunne's second dream was almost as nightmarish. In it he was walking along a pathway between two fields, with 3-metre-high iron fencing on each side. Suddenly in the field to his left a huge horse began to kick and plunge as if it had gone mad. Dunne glanced around to make sure the animal couldn't get through the fence, then walked on. But almost at once he heard the horse thundering along the path behind him. He ran towards some wooden steps that he hoped would let him escape and had almost reached them when he woke up.

The following day he was fishing with his brother when he realised he was looking at the scene from his dream. There were the fields, there was the path, there were the wooden steps (leading to a bridge) and there, to his horror, was the lunatic horse, kicking and jumping just as before. Once again Dunne looked for gaps in the fencing to make sure he and his brother were safe. Once again there were none. But once again the animal somehow broke free and thundered down the path. It eventually plunged into the river, then galloped off along a road.

What began to fascinate Dunne was the way these dreams *distorted* their predictions of the future. The first was quite clearly about the French fire that killed so many factory workers, but that wasn't what he'd actually dreamed. For example, he'd dreamed that he was there, right in the middle of the whole event, whereas in reality it took place a long way away. He'd also seen a board platform,

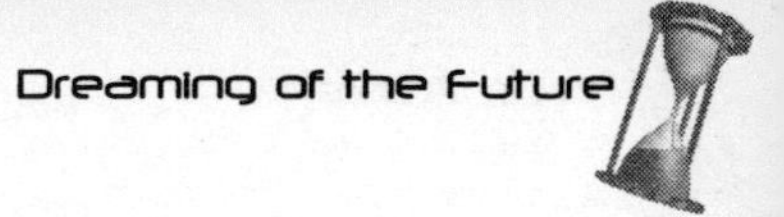

whereas the real tragedy occurred on a properly made balcony.

Distortions were even more obvious in the second dream. The fields he saw were larger in his dream than they were in reality, as was the lunatic horse. The high metal fencing in his dream was replaced in reality by much lower wooden railings. In his dream the horse was in the left-hand field. In reality it was in the right. And Dunne himself was never on the path, nor was he chased by the horse.

This led him to conclude that even his most predictive dreams weren't exactly visions of the future. He began to study the whole process of dreaming and found psychologists agreed that dreams were stitched together from your experiences in waking life – often presented in symbolic form. You might, for example, have a terrible row with your mother because she wouldn't let you go to a pop concert, then dream that an old witch locked you up in a dungeon while minstrels played merrily outside.

What struck Dunne forcibly from his own

experience was that it wasn't just past events that produced such dreams. Some of them seemed to be influenced by events that didn't occur for days, sometimes weeks and even years after the dream itself.

The second unexpected discovery Dunne made was that he wasn't alone. In a paper published in the *Journal of the American Society for Psychical Research*[6], Dr Mary S. Stowell described how she analysed 51 apparently predictive dreams and discovered 37 of them were subsequently confirmed as accurate – well beyond any question of coincidence or chance. (One dreamer witnessed a plane crash in a specific location, told her husband about the dream the following morning, then watched news reports of the same crash, in the same place, just a few weeks later.)

The dreams investigated by Dr Stowell were clearly recalled by those who had them, but literally thousands of others have had the same type of predictive dreams as Dunne did ... and never even noticed. You might even be one of them.

[6] Vol 91:p163, 1997, as reported by William Corless in *Science Frontiers*, The Sourcebook Project, Michigan, 2000.

Chapter 12

Dream Travel

Ask around and you'll soon find people who claim they never dream. You'll find even more who claim they only dream occasionally. You may even think that about yourself, but if you do ... you're wrong.

Everybody, without exception, dreams every night, except in cases of high fever. As a baby, you dreamed for about half the time you were asleep – now it's somewhere between a fifth and a quarter. If you manage to survive beyond 65, there'll be a slight increase in your dreaming time, although you won't revert to the high dream rate of childhood. We know all this because of something called Rapid Eye Movements – REM for short.

Back in 1953, sleep scientists (and yes, there really are such things) noticed that, about an hour and a half after falling asleep, laboratory subjects started moving their eyes back and forth under closed lids as if they were watching a tennis match. At the same time, their brainwave pattern reverted to that of an alert, waking person.

So the scientists woke the subjects up and asked them what was going on. Almost all of them said they'd been dreaming.

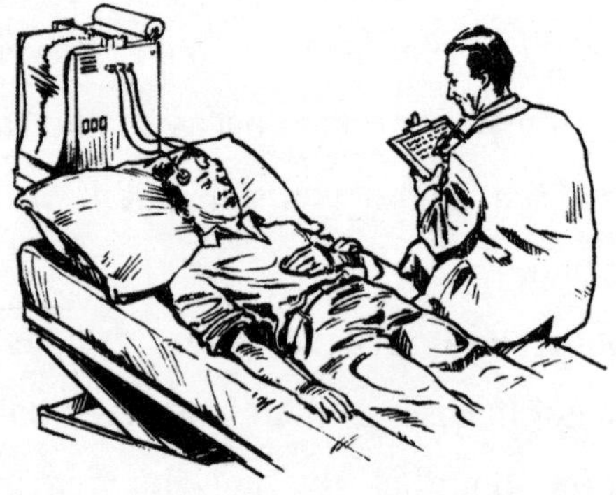

Assuming you're in good health, you'll normally have about four separate periods of dreaming every night. These gradually increase in length until towards the end of the night you're dreaming more or less constantly. Although dreams occur in colour, they often fade to black and white when you remember them. Except, of course, that most times you *don't* remember them. Which is why so many

people believe they never dream at all; and why so many more never realise they've been dreaming about the future.

If you're interested in finding out whether your mind travels through time at night, the first thing you have to do is learn to remember your dreams. This isn't easy, particularly at first, but after a while it becomes a habit and suddenly a whole new world of experience opens up to you.

Here's how to start: first, take a notebook and pen to bed with you. (If you're a techie, a cassette recorder is even better, provided you're alone in the room. If you share a room with a brother or sister they'll not thank you for waking them in the middle of the night by muttering into a microphone.) A small pad is best and if you can find one of those fancy pens that include a tiny torch, that would be really brilliant.

Leave the gear – pen and pad or recorder – on your bedside table where you can reach them easily without knocking over your glass of water or bedside lamp. Next, as you prepare yourself for sleep, tell yourself aloud that you are going to

remember your dreams tonight. You'll feel silly, but talking firmly to yourself really does help. Then forget your worries, get your head down and go to sleep.

Every time you wake up, during the night or in the morning, write down or record your last dream *at once*. And I really mean *at once*. This is by far the most important trick in dream recall. If you wait even a few seconds, the dream will start to fade; a few more and it disappears completely. So even though you're going to be sorely tempted to roll over and curl up in that nice warm bed just a minute more, *resist!* Grab the pen, grab the pad and get the dream down on paper *at once*.

You're not likely to remember all your dreams, even if you wake up several times through the night. But don't let that worry you. Catch as many as you can. When you're starting out, you should force yourself to write down every detail of every dream. You'll quickly find that very few dreams obey the rules of waking life. Events blend into each other. You can find yourself moving instantaneously from one place to another. Impossible things happen. Don't try to make sense of any of this. Just record everything you remember, however peculiar.

Later on, as you get used to working with your dreams and your memory of them improves, you can make life a little easier by just taking notes through the night. But always write them up fully afterwards. You'll discover in a minute why *details* are important.

You may find from time to time that you simply can't remember your dream. If that happens, return at once to the position you were in at the exact moment of waking. I don't know why, but this will often get your memory working again. If it doesn't, then try this:

1. Ask yourself whether the dream was pleasant or unpleasant?

2. Were any of your friends in it?

3. Did it take place in a town or in the country?

4. Did it have a particular theme?

5. What was the overall shape of the dream?

6. What was the 'feel' of the dream?

With luck, this will start the dream flooding back. But catching your dreams is only the first step. You need to write each one up fully in a dream journal you keep specially for the purpose. Date each dream – this is important – and hide the journal away carefully. (If you think other people might stumble on it, you'll start making changes in your dreams, cutting out the naughty bits and so on, which is the last thing you need.)

As your dream journal begins to build, you can start searching through it for predictive dreams. Like John Dunne, you may find some of your dreams will come true within a day or two. But keep going back to the beginning of your dream journal and re-read the whole record frequently, because some dreams can predict events that take weeks, months or even years to come about.

If you're very lucky, you'll find yourself having dreams like those I described in the last chapter and it will be obvious what events they predict. But mostly you won't and this is where John Dunne's discoveries come into play.

After years of studying his own dreams and those of many people who carried out similar experiments, Dunne decided that dreams were fantasies your unconscious mind made up using bits and pieces of your waking experience. A dream would typically draw on something you did, something you said, something you felt.

So far, Dunne's ideas match those of most psychologists, but he went on to add a vital factor: the events your mind uses to create dream

fantasies can occur in your future just as easily as in your past. Your sleeping mind, Dunne came to believe, roamed around your past, present and your future gathering material for your nightly entertainments. But even more important is the fact that your dream will often present the experience *in symbolic form.*

For example, in one of the dreams Dunne collected, a man dreamed he was outside in the open air when people began to throw lighted cigarettes at his face. In his dream he stood terrified as burning cigarettes streamed towards him. A week or so later, he was outside sawing up some wood using a circular saw. Unnoticed by him,

one plank had a nail in it and as the saw hit the nail, sparks streamed towards his face.

In this instance, the experience of the stream of sparks was symbolised in the dream by people throwing lighted cigarettes. There are lots of books available about the way dreams convert waking events into symbols and a little study will help you recognise what your mind gets up to at night. And if you keep careful track in your dream journal, you could easily find that one of the things it gets up to is a little time travel.

Chapter 13

The Science of Time Travel

All the same, dreaming is a far cry from the sort of time travel H. G. Wells wrote about, the sort we examined briefly right back at the beginning of this book where you press a button and *physically* go back and forth in time. Could something of that sort actually be possible?

Some of our case studies might suggest it is, but it's hard to be absolutely sure. Arnold Toynbee certainly *felt* as if he'd slipped through time, but maybe his experiences were hallucinations, or some sort of waking dreams. Jane O'Neill thought her trip to ancient Fotheringhay was a past-life vision. The vision theory seems a little strained when two or more people share the same experience, like the Victorian schoolmistresses at Versailles or the naval cadets at Kersey. Yet Malcolm Turner's Roman orgy

(confirmed at least in part by his wife) wasn't as solid as it might have been – he put his hand right through the shoulder of one Roman.

So would *real* time travel, the sort where you actually, physically, move through time contradict the laws of physics? The surprising answer is no; and the man who says so is the greatest physicist of the last 100 years, Albert Einstein.

Einstein blew the whistle on the common sense idea of time way back in 1905 when he reached some interesting conclusions on a problem that had been troubling physicists since 1887. To understand the problem, consider the following.

You're standing at one end of a 6-kilometre- (10-mile-) long racetrack. There's a photographer's flash gun set up at the other. When the flash goes off light starts rushing towards you at 290,000 kilometres (186,000 miles) a second. Freeze that situation in your imagination, then look at the following alternative situations.

1. As the flash goes off, you use your hitherto unsuspected super powers to run *towards* the flash gun at (170,000 kilometres) 100,000 miles a second.

2. As the flash goes off, you use your super powers to run *away from* the flash gun at (170,000 kilometres)100,000 miles a second.

Common sense (and Newtonian physics) will tell you that in the first case, the light is bound to reach you earlier than in the second. But in 1887, two scientists (Edward Morley and Albert Michelson) carried out an experiment that proved without doubt the light reaches you at exactly the same time in both cases: doesn't matter if you're running towards it or running away.

Scientists went out of their minds trying to find out where Morley and Michelson went wrong, but without success. Then Einstein came along and said, in effect, what happens if they weren't wrong? What happens if it's common sense that's wrong? The result was his two Theories of Relativity, which dealt largely with gravity but had the side effect of changing the way science thought of time forever. To begin with, Einstein ditched Newton's notion that time was a thing in itself, somehow measuring events from outside the universe. In its place he put forward the idea that time was a sort of *direction.* You already had the three dimensions of space – length, breadth and thickness – but suppose, Einstein thought, there was another direction you could measure, a fourth dimension of space. And suppose that fourth dimension was hidden from us because we didn't *experience* it as a direction. Suppose we experienced it as the *passing of time.*

This meant time wasn't something outside space, but a part of space itself. And since time was now an aspect of space, he decided it didn't make sense to label them separately, so he coined the term Spacetime (or the Spacetime continuum) to describe the totality of the universe as we know it.

This idea had implications for anybody interested in time travel. The past may feel as if it's lost and gone forever, but if Einstein was right, all events of every age are actually a part of spacetime. You and

I travel through our own little area of spacetime in what's usually a one-way trip. And since you're currently reading this book, your little area of spacetime overlaps on mine.

But the *idea* of spacetime was only the start. Einstein needed to prove his theory mathematically and since he wasn't very good at mathematics, he asked his old schoolteacher – a man named Herman Minowski – to do the sums for him. The result was the Minowski Equations, a set of formulae that show the whole of your past and the whole of your future must and do meet at a single point.

That point is the eternal *now* of spacetime and it has a specific location. It always exists at the exact position you're at now: all your past, all your future comes together at the instant you read these words on the exact spot *where* you read them.

You can change your location in space without destroying the universe. The whole forwards/backwards meeting of your future and your past moves with you. But the real question is, can you change your location in time?

Chapter 14

Lifeworms

Getting your head around Einstein's idea of a four-dimensional spacetime isn't easy. But there are a couple of images that may help. Although you naturally think of yourself as a person who was once born and will sometime die, the theory of four-dimensional spacetime suggests such a viewpoint is really an illusion. If you could somehow pull back, you would see yourself as a very alien being indeed – a gigantic worm-like creature tapering to an embryo at one end, decaying as a corpse at the other and meandering through the three spacial dimensions in between.

This lifeworm is interconnected with all your ancestral lifeworms, which still exist, don't forget, in the massive spacetime continuum. That tapered embryo is actually buried inside the lifeworm structure of your mother, who is tapered inside her mother and so on in an interlocking web that stretches vast distances back to the original mother of us all.

If you think through this picture carefully, you'll note that your ancestral web connects with the webs of others until it becomes obvious that the entire human race is a single, interlocking body, spread through the continuum to an extent at which we can only guess.

This is a mind-numbing picture, but another image will help you come to grips with it. You've probably seen at least one time-lapse photo of an athlete in a race. At one side there's the athlete crouched on his starting blocks. At the other, he's breasting the finishing tape. But in between there's a whole series of blurred images: he's rising out of the starting position ... taking his first step ... leaning forward as he gathers momentum ... and so on.

Each of these blurred images shows the athlete in the process of running. Each has been plucked out, so to speak, from the act. But the photograph as a whole shows the athlete's extension through time – at least for the duration of the race.

Your whole life is like a much larger version of that time-lapse picture. The various events you think of as lying in your future are, in a sense, already in place and have been from the day of your conception, as part of the complete four-dimensional being you are.

That's not the way it feels, of course. You don't sense time as an extension of space, whatever Einstein says. What you experience is a sort of motion along the time dimension, a *growing into* that enormous lifeworm. Your awareness spearheads this growth, always presenting you with what you think of as the present moment.

There's no real movement in time at all, but the focus of your awareness makes you think there is. It's like sitting in a train and watching the scenery flash by. We all know the scenery doesn't really move at all ... but it certainly seems to.

And it may even be I'm completely wrong in saying that your lifeworm is fully in place from the moment of your conception. We both know you didn't start out fully extended in *three*-dimensional space. You were once a microscopic cell that started to divide and kept dividing, then grew and grew until you reached the size you are today. Maybe your extension in the time dimension is like that as well. Maybe it starts small and grows.

But on the face of things, the evidence seems to be against it. The theory of the pre-existing (fully extended) lifeworm goes a long way towards explaining the mechanism behind John Dunne's peculiar dreams. If your mind can wander back along your lifeworm (in the form of memory) to find material for your dreams, a fully extended lifeworm would permit memories of the future as well.

The Minowski Equations seem to suggest that while time travel may be possible, you can't travel in both time and *space during the same journey. In other words, if you want to watch the pyramids being built, you must first journey to the Giza Plateau in Egypt,* then *travel back in time. Or, alternatively, travel back in time wherever you happen to be,* then *make your way to Egypt.*

What you can't do is start out at, say, Charing Cross Station and travel directly back in time to the first stone-laying of the pyramids.

But whatever about the equations, experiences like those of Arnold Toynbee (see chapter 4 on The Man Who Witnessed History) seem to contradict the conclusion.

Which is exactly what dreams in general – and Dunne's dreams in particular – seem to show. The sleeping cinema show takes in memories from both directions and it's interesting to note Dunne never predicted anything from the distant future: only things he experienced personally or through reading about them in a newspaper.

Chapter 15

Flatland

All the same, there have been a few people whose dreams of the future went beyond their own lifetimes. One of them was the 16th century French prophet Michel de Nostradame – better known as Nostradamus.

In his day, Nostradamus wrote down several hundred prophecies, many of them so obscure you could attach them to almost anything. But among the dross were some so detailed that they clearly referred to a specific event. For example, he described the death of the French King Henry II so vividly that his queen commanded him to the palace to explain the prophecy. When it came true, there were demonstrations against Nostradamus in the streets, as if he were somehow to blame for what he'd foreseen.

That prediction was in line with Dunne's experience of dreams, since Nostradamus lived to see it come to pass. But some of his other prophecies placed him in an entirely different league. The best known of them referred to a particular – and quite unique – political event: the famous 'Flight to Varennes' by the French king Louis XVI.

At the height of the French Revolution, King Louis decided to flee the country with his wife, Marie Antoinette. They commandeered a carriage. Marie Antoinette dressed in her finest white gown, Louis chose more sober grey clothes. Then they made for the border by a roundabout route that took them to the town of Varennes where they expected a change of horses. Their coachman failed to find the horses (which had been left at the other side of the town) and spent so much time looking for them that the King was recognised and his

presence reported to a Monsieur Saulce, a local oil merchant who was also an official of the newly formed Revolutionary Commune.

Saulce alerted the National Assembly and Louis was ordered to return to the capital. Shortly after he did so, a 500-strong mob invaded his Tuileries Palace and forced the King to wear the Revolution's red cap of liberty. The political situation worsened. The King's Minister, Comte de Narbonne was sacked and replaced by a revolutionary. Eventually, in a terrible bloodbath, both Louis and Marie Antoinette were beheaded on the guillotine.

In prophecies describing these events, Nostradamus accurately dated the French Revolution, foresaw the adoption of a revolutionary calendar, predicted the exact length of time the Christian Church was persecuted. He specifically mentioned the town of Varennes, the roundabout route by which it was reached, the presence of the King and Queen, what they were both wearing and the fact that Louis was an elected leader, the first in human history.

He went on to mention M. Saulce by name (and the fact that he was a supplier of oil) then described the invasion of the Tuileries by a crowd of 500, the crowning of the King with the liberty cap and the loss of Narbonne's title. Finally, he predicted that the end result would be 'bloody slicing'.

This massive amount of detail leaves no room for doubt that he accurately foresaw the French Revolution. Yet Nostradamus was born in 1503 and died in 1556 which, from the perspective of four-dimensional spacetime, made him a

53-year-long lifeworm snaking its way through France with occasional brief spacial extensions into neighbouring countries.

This may have allowed him to project his awareness to examine events along his own timeline, as Dunne clearly managed, but doesn't explain how he was able to gather so many details of an event that occurred some 230 years after his lifeworm ended. For that, you need to take a very different view on spacetime.

Oddly enough, one excellent way to get a grip on spacetime with its three dimensions of space and one dimension of time is to imagine how the world would look if you were only aware of two dimensions of space and not the third – in other words, imagine Flatland.

In Flatland, 'flat-you' can only ever see objects that have two dimensions: length and breadth, but never height. The third dimension exists all right – it's just that your limited flat senses can never actually perceive it. When you come across a cube, for example, all you can see is a square. The extension of the square into the third dimension is

quite invisible to you and can't be touched or sensed in any other way.

Flatland has some very curious properties. Assume for a moment that you are a dot crawling around it. If you run into a line from the side, it acts as a barrier to your progress, exactly like a fence or a wall in the three-dimensional world. You have to find the end of the line to get around it. Meet with the same line end-on and at first it looks like a dot, just like you. It's only on closer examination that you'll discover it's actually a line.

If the Flatland police want to put you in jail, all they have to do is draw a circle around you. As long as they don't leave a gap, there's no way you can get out.

Interestingly, if you have a god-like friend in the third dimension who rescues you by lifting you up out of the circle, this will appear to the Flatland police as something of a miracle. One minute you were safely confined inside their circle, the next you disappeared (into the third dimension, but they can't know that) only to reappear outside the circle as your 3-D friend sets you down again.

Since there is absolutely nothing in the physics of Flatland to explain this, Flatland sceptics will deny it ever happened at all. They will accuse the police of hallucinating and dismiss similar reports as myth. Once you get accustomed to thinking about Flatland, it becomes a very useful tool for examining your real four-dimensional spacetime continuum. Just as 'fat-you' couldn't sense the third dimension of space, 'flat-you' can't directly sense the fourth. Nobody you know can look along the direction of time to see what's coming: our senses just don't work like that.

But maybe every so often somebody is born whose senses *do* work that way. Maybe there are a very few people who can literally see along the timeline into the future. And maybe Nostradamus was one of them. Perhaps some inherited characteristic or weird technique allowed him a glance beyond his lifeworm in the fourth-dimensional direction and his attention was briefly caught by the political upheaval that were to change the political face of his country and the world.

Chapter 16

Travel to the Future

Although Nostradamus can teach us something about the nature of time, his real talent wasn't time travel – not even mental time travel. It was more like good eyesight. And so far, all our examples of genuine physical time travel have involved people apparently moving from the present to the past – to the time of Louis XVI, the Middle Ages, the Roman occupation of Britain or whenever. But Einstein's insights soon showed time travel in the other direction was equally possible. The background to this is a bit tricky to explain, but stick with me because it gets a whole lot easier in a paragraph or two.

If you want to find out the speed of any moving object – car, train, plane or cricket ball – you need to make two measurements: the time it takes and the distance it has to cover. In other words, you need a clock and a ruler. The trouble starts when you try to use your clock and your ruler to measure the speed of light – you find it's always the same whether you're moving away from the source, moving towards the source or standing still. We know that's what you'll find because it's what Morley and Michelson *did* find (see chapter 13).

Since that doesn't make any sense, Einstein argued that if the speed of light doesn't change, then your measuring instruments – your clock and your ruler – change. In other words, a constant speed of light can only be the result of rulers growing shorter and clocks running slower if they happen to be moving. (The way it works is that your ruler gets shorter so light has less distance to travel along it and your clock runs slower so light has more time to make the trip.)

Did you catch that? If your clock and ruler are moving, the clock runs slower and the ruler gets shorter. What's more, the clock doesn't run slower because movement affects the mechanism. It runs slower because *time itself* is running slower. And if

you find it hard to understand how something as substantial as a ruler can get shorter try imagining what happens when a large squashy balloon meets a headwind. The balloon not only slows down because of the headwind, but it also starts to flatten – it's a bit like that with the ruler.

You might wonder why you never noticed this yourself. The answer is you just don't move fast enough. But that doesn't mean it doesn't happen. In 1972, four super-accurate atomic clocks were loaded onto an aeroplane, while four more – all carefully synchronised – were left on the ground. The plane then took off on a round-the-world flight. When it got back, comparison showed the clocks on the plane were running ever so slightly behind the clocks that were left behind. Later, the same experiment was carried out using space rockets. The results were even more pronounced. Einstein's bright idea has been tested and proved to be right on the nail.

And that, as Einstein himself showed, means that with a fast enough spaceship, you could fly right into the future. To get far enough into the future

so you'd actually notice, you'd need something faster than the spaceships on offer as I write. The best we have (for a round trip) is NASA's Space Shuttle, which cruises around 26,500 km/h (16,500 mph); and that won't hack it. But suppose some

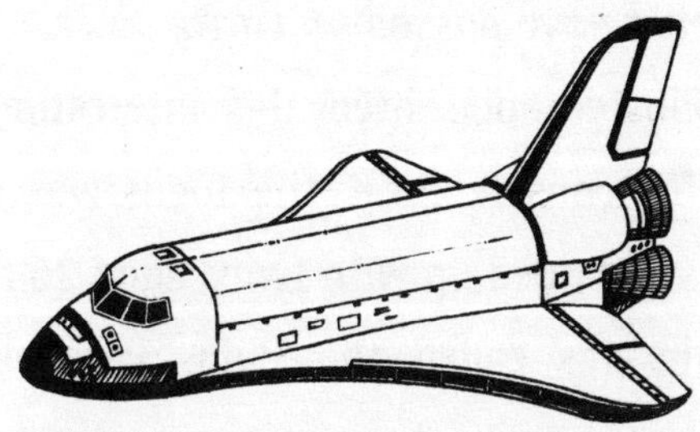

bright engineer invents a drive that's powered by muons. Muons are particles smaller than an atom that travel at 99% the speed of light. At that speed, scientists have discovered, time slows to one-seventh its normal rate.

So here's how you fly into the future, according to Einstein who worked it all out in what he called his Twins Paradox. You start with a pair of twins, both (obviously!) 30 years old. One works as an astronaut for NASA, the other runs a corner shop. The astronaut twin takes off on a five-year mission in a muon-driven spaceship travelling at 99% the speed of light.

Remember what that means: time on the spaceship is running seven times slower than it does back on Earth. When the ship completes its round trip and comes home, five years has passed on board so the astronaut twin is now 35 years old. *But 35 years have passed on Earth.*

When Einstein presented this interesting little scenario for consideration, the focus was on the fact that you ended up with twins aged 35 and 65. (That's why it's called the Twins Paradox.) But thinking about twins diverts your attention from what actually happens here.

It's not just the twin at home who gets older – everything on Earth is that much older as well. On Earth, 35 years has passed for just five years on the spaceship. In other words, the astronaut has flown 35 years into the future.

Although all the spontaneous time slips quoted so far in this book have involved people moving into the past, there is one case of a slip in the opposite direction.

In 1935, Air-Marshal Sir Victor Goddard (then still just a Wing Commander) visited a disused airfield at Drem near Edinburgh in Scotland. The tarmac of the runways was broken and cracked, with cattle grazing on grass that had forced its way through. But just hours later when he flew back to Drem, the airfield had been completely renovated and was in full use with mechanics walking around and planes on the runway. One of these was a model he couldn't even recognise.

Four years later he solved the mystery. With war now raging in Europe, he visited Drem again and found it exactly as he had seen it in 1935, complete with blue-overalled mechanics and yellow planes. He even found the plane he had been unable to identify– a Miles Magister.

Muons are pretty nippy little things, but it's possible to imagine – as many science-fiction writers already have – that an engine might be developed that would power a spaceship even faster ... say 99.9% the speed of light. In that sort of situation, astronauts wouldn't just fly 35 years into the future, they'd travel centuries, perhaps millennia.

If an astronaut had a twin brother or sister, the twin would be long dead. The astronaut might meet her own descendants, many generations removed. She could see how the world turned out, learn what civilisations rose and fell. She could, in fact, do much the same thing H. G. Wells' time traveller did when he pointed his machine towards the distant future. Except for one thing, of course. She couldn't come back.

Chapter 17

Black Holes

The trouble with using sheer speed to propel yourself into the future is that it has its limits. With the right sort of technology, you might push your spaceship close to the speed of light, but you could never push it faster.

Einstein's calculations showed that not only did your ruler (spaceship or whatever) get shorter the faster it travelled, but it also increased in mass. Once again, this hardly shows up when you're in a racing car or even a jet plane, but as you approach the speed of light, the effect gets more and more pronounced. At the speed of light, your mass becomes infinite.

What this means (if physicists have got their maths right) that if you take the Relativity formulae at face value, the faster you push your

spaceship, the slower time runs and the more massive the ship gets until, at the speed of light, time stops altogether. Your craft is now so massive it fills the entire universe ... and then some. Clearly that's the end of the line and the reason why Einstein maintained you can never accelerate anything faster than the speed of light.

Having said that, some of his fellow physicists pointed out that there might exist a few things in the universe that were already travelling faster than the speed of light so acceleration didn't come into it. This led to the study of particles called *tachyons* (these can only be studied in theory as no one has ever found one), which proved to have some very weird properties. For one thing, the less energy they have, the faster tachyons will go – in other words, you have to push it forward to slow it down. But the most interesting thing about tachyons is that every one of them would travel back in time.

As yet, nobody has proved tachyons exist – that's to say, nobody has ever actually found one – but most physicists believe they probably do. This is something that's over excited science-fiction writers who frequently invent timeships with tachyon drives, conveniently forgetting that before you and I can catch up with a tachyon, we have to achieve zero time and infinite mass without getting confused or doing damage to our internal organs.

All the same, if you somehow *could* go as fast as a tachyon, it would solve the problem highlighted at the end of the last chapter. If racing towards the speed of light propels you into the future, racing faster than the speed of light would certainly bring you back again. But even leaving aside this unlikely possibility, there was another aspect of the Relativity Theories that held some promise for the time traveller. This was Einstein's discovery that the presence of matter – a star, a planet, a moon or even your big toe – distorts the fabric of spacetime.

As you might guess, your big toe doesn't distort it very much, but by the time you get to something as big as a planet or even a decent-sized moon, the effect on spacetime is so obvious that we can feel it. We experience it as gravitational pull.

The distortion of spacetime caused by your average star is very pronounced indeed – more than enough to kill you if you got too close. And there are some stars so massive that they don't just twist spacetime; they rip it apart. What you get then is a Black Hole.

Black Holes started out as mathematical calculations in physicists' notebooks, but after a while astronomers started to get in on the act. In 1932, a Russian scientist called Lev Landau, came up with the idea of a neutron star, a body so tightly packed that if our Sun was one, it would measure less than 20 kilometres (13 miles) across. In 1967, two British astronomers – Jocelyn Bell and Antony Hewish – found one.

Neutron stars are formed when an ordinary star is too big to hold up its own weight. Although the pressures of its nuclear furnace can keep it burning big and brightly for a while, there eventually comes a time when it starts to collapse in on itself, becoming smaller and smaller, more and more dense, until it becomes a neutron star.

neutron star

But if the star is *really* big to begin with, it doesn't stop there. It keeps on collapsing, smaller and smaller until, at a certain point, it isn't a star any more – it's a Black Hole. (If our Sun was big enough – which it isn't – it would make a Black Hole just over 3 kilometres [2 miles] across.) You may have begun to wonder what all this has to do with time travel, but stick with me: Black Holes have some interesting properties.

An Australian physicist by the name of Roy Kerr

did the mathematical mapping of spinning Black Holes. He showed there were two event horizons (points at which escape velocity equals the speed of light) one inside the other. He also discovered that when you pass through the first of these, space and time switch places. The only way you can move in space is in the direction of the pull, but when you get to this point you can move in time any way you want. Which means there are parts of a Black Hole where you can travel in time as easily as you now stroll down a street. But Black Holes are dangerous places – you'd be crushed by their gravity long before you reached this point – so maybe there's an easier way.

Chapter 18

The Time Machine

In 1974, an American physicist called Frank Tipler published plans for the world's first working time machine. He didn't call it a time machine in the title. His paper (published in the scientific journal *Physical Review*) was called 'Rotating Cylinders and the Possibility of Global Causality Violation' which doesn't give much of a clue to what it was all about. But what it was all about was a path that winds through space and turns around in time.

The path Tipler wrote about was called a 'closed timelike-line,' something that came up in the mathematics of Relativity Theory. The formulae predicted the possibility of a track that would take you through spacetime, but twisted in a way that brought you back to where *and when* you started.

When you get right down to it, maths are just little signs on paper, but it's fun trying to imagine what they might mean in the real world. If you found a closed timelike-line – behind the bicycle shed, for example – you could stroll off and get into all sorts of mischief, but nobody outside the path would even notice you'd gone because you'd get back again, dirty and exhausted, at the exact second you left. The question, of course, has always been whether a closed timelike-line could actually exist in the real world.

It probably sounded a lot less weird to scientists in the 1970s than it does to you today. Back then quite a few of them more or less accepted the possibility of time travel, based on Einstein's discovery that a big enough mass warped the spacetime continuum. (These things follow fashions. By the time the late 1980s and 1990s rolled around, the world-famous Cambridge physicist Stephen Hawking had decided time travel *wasn't* possible and never would be. By 2002, he'd changed his mind and decided it might be after all.)

But in the 1970s, you still had physicists who

hadn't given up on Black Holes. One of them, Hans Moravac, thought that even if you couldn't get through one, you might peer into it to see the future. And closed timelike-lines were very closely associated with Black Holes. The maths showed they would exist if a Black Hole was spinning, although you'd have to fly through the Black Hole twice to complete the loop.

Closed timelike-lines were also associated with something called wormholes, a term familiar to every follower of *Star Trek* and in particular *Star Trek: Deep Space Nine*, a series set on a space station that guarded a massive wormhole giving access to a very distant part of the galaxy.

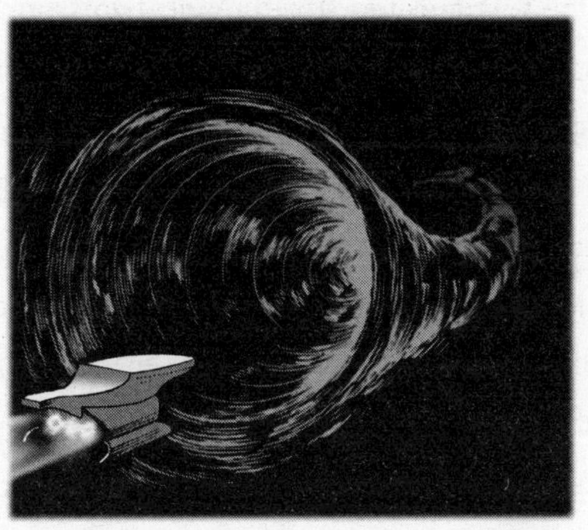

The writers of *Star Trek* got it partly right and partly wrong. What they got right was that wormholes are (in theory) tunnels drilling through spacetime to connect widely separated areas of the universe. What they got wrong was that if wormholes really do exist in the universe they're only likely to be usable by worms – and extremely small, fast worms at that. Wormholes big enough to take a spaceship, or even big enough to stick your arm through, don't really fit the maths. What's more they only exist for a fraction of a second. By the time you've spotted one it's gone.

Having said that, wormholes do tend to pick up closed timelike-lines, although you'd have to breathe out and squeeze through two wormholes to get back to the same universe you left, let alone the same place and time.

So you couldn't use a Black Hole timelike-line because it would kill you, and you couldn't use a wormhole timelike-line because wormholes are too small and short-lived. But when it came to timelike-lines, Frank Tipler had a really bright idea – he wondered if you mightn't simply make one.

And the way to make one was to build a big enough rotating cylinder. Once you had that, you had yourself a time machine.

The time machine Tipler had in mind was a whole lot different from the time machine (above) H. G. Wells wrote about. There were no cogs and gears, no gyroscopes, no rotating discs, no steering wheels, no seat. In its place, you had a large spinning cylinder that warped space. It was the centre point of the warped region that was the time machine, because it contained the closed

timelike-line.

Which meant you could start out with your transport vehicle anywhere outside the zone, fly in, move backwards or forwards in time, then return to your original spacetime coordinates: back where and when you started from. That was what got Tipler's fellow-physicists excited. With Black Holes and wormholes and every other means of time travel anybody had so far thought of, the trip had to be out of control. You could travel to the past all right, but whether you ever got to see the pyramid-builders was a matter of dumb luck. You could travel to the future, but you couldn't control whether you jumped five minutes or five million years. And either way, coming back was the real nightmare. Your chances of ever returning to your own time, even give or take several thousand years, were vanishingly small.

But following a closed timelike-line, like the one generated by Frank Tipler's machine, guaranteed you made it back right on the button. You could even save yourself a little time by coming back before you left. With something like a Black Hole, you had to take what you got. But Frank Tipler's machine was specially designed to maximise the time travel effect – and do it in a way that could actually be used by frail, spacefaring human beings. The principle was quite straightforward: if you make your cylinder big enough and dense enough, then set it spinning fast enough, it will warp spacetime in a specific way.

The way it warps spacetime is 'sinusoid', a term used to describe anything that swings or bends to return to its original state, like the pendulum of a grandfather clock. Tipler's pendulum, however, is the swing of time itself. The cylinder he proposed

would make time swing back and forth. Catch one swing and you move back in time. Catch another and you move forward.

The swings themselves form clearly defined zones in ordinary space. Aim your spacecraft into one with care and you should become a time traveller without getting ripped apart by the forces of gravity that cause the warp.

Chapter 19

Building Your Own Time Machine

Frank Tipler's 1974 paper explained the theory of his time machine, but stopped short of explaining how one might be built. The practical problems are, quite frankly, immense.

Start with the basic cylinder. When Tipler said it had to be massive enough to warp spacetime, he meant *really* massive. So much so you wouldn't have the room to set it up on Earth. That means you have to build it in space – but not inside the solar system. The gravitational forces it would produce are so immense they would influence the movements of the planets round the Sun. So you have to ship your construction team and all their materials into outer space, well away from our

planet, our Sun or anything else it might damage.

And those materials would be a problem in themselves. You couldn't, for example, make the cylinder from plastic or steel. To get enough mass, you'd need more of those raw materials than there are in our entire galaxy. In fact the only stuff you could use would be atomic nuclei: little specks of matter so dense that a teaspoonful of them weighs around a billion tonnes.

Since we can't ship men and materials outside the solar system and we haven't the remotest idea how to extract nucleic material, you might be tempted to dismiss a Tipler Cylinder as impossible. But you need to be careful here. When engineers say something is impossible, they can mean one of two things. The first is that it's *absolutely* impossible, because what you're trying to do contradicts a fundamental law of nature, like picking yourself up by the laces of your trainers. With this sort of impossibility, you know it will never happen, however clever the human race gets and however many marvellous laces we invent.

The second meaning is that it's *technically*

impossible, which simply says there's no way we can do it *yet.* Building a Ferrari was impossible in the Stone Age: we didn't have the metal for the bodywork, the rubber for the tyres, the plastic for the battery or the know-how to put them all together even if somebody had presented us with all the bits. But that only implies a Ferrari was impossible back *then.* Given time and technical advances the car was built and painted red and has been threatening speed limits ever since.

Tipler's time machine is like that. We can't build it today and we probably won't be able to build it in the next century or so, but there's nothing in the design that contradicts any basic law of nature, so it remains only a technical impossibility. One day, we might manage it. Physicist Fred Alan Wolf has even figured out how.

Fred's bright idea – as ingenious in its own way as Tipler's original theory – is to use neutron stars. If you've been paying close attention earlier in this book, you'll know that a neutron star is a stellar body that's collapsed in on itself, but hasn't quite made it all the way to becoming a Black Hole. All

the same, it's managed something very spectacular. The electrons inside its very atoms have been plunged into their core where they fuse with protons to become neutrons. Then the atoms themselves fuse together until the entire star is effectively one gigantic atomic nucleus. The stuff it's made of is just the ticket if you want to build a Tipler cylinder.

All the same, mining it might prove difficult. Neutron stars are tiny – not much larger than a planet in most cases – but their gravitational pull is immense. You and I couldn't even stand on Jupiter without getting flattened, so what chance would we have with a pickaxe on a neutron star? A better idea might be to use the whole star.

The key to creating a time machine that could actually be used by humans (as opposed to a Black Hole which offers lethal time gates) is to build a cylinder so long that it generates time travel zones far enough away from its rotating surface to allow human access without the inconvenience of being crushed by gravity. To do that, you'll need a cylinder 4,000 kilometres (2,480 miles) long and maybe 40 kilometres (25 miles) across, all made from neutron star stuff. That'll use up about 100 neutron stars.

You'll have to find some way of pushing them together, but that's only technically impossible today, not absolutely impossible for all time. If you do it carefully enough, you'll automatically solve the problem of spinning your cylinder. The point here is that most neutron stars are *already* rotating on their axes at about the rate of spin you'll need to produce your time field. If you shunt them together so their spins are synchronised, then your whole daisy-chain cylinder of stars comes into being – ready to rock and roll.

Chapter 20

Flying Through Time

To fly through time, you have to approach a Tipler cylinder end on. Any other way and you'll be sucked down onto the surface of the cylinder itself and squashed, along with your spaceship, like an annoying gnat. Even if some ingenious anti-gravity technology helped you avoid this fate, any approach at an angle to the axis of the spin leaves you unable to reach the time zones generated by the cylinder. They only exist, in the form of rings, when you fly in, straight and true, from the side. But get the angle right and this is what you will be facing:

The Cylinder and the Zones

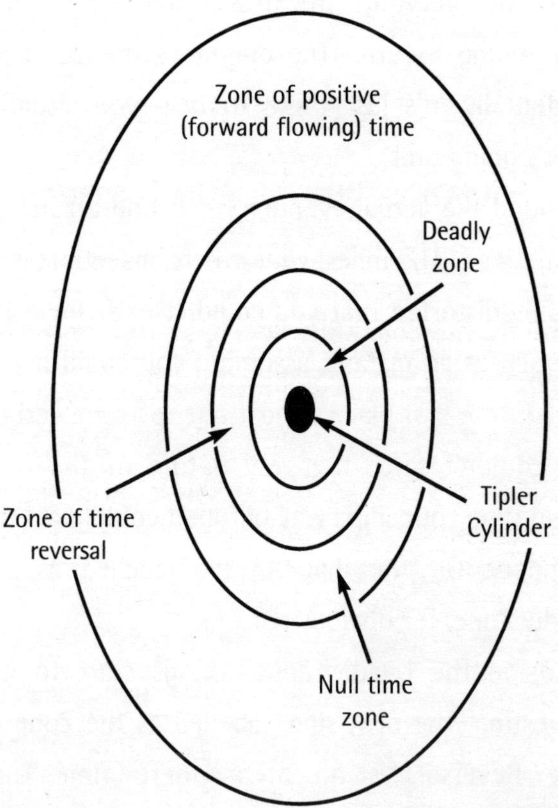

Right in the middle there is the Tipler Cylinder itself, viewed end-on, perfectly visible since neutron stars still shine (although not as brightly as they once did) and endlessly spinning at a rate that's a percentage of the speed of light. Around it

are what appear to be a series of clearly defined rings of varying thickness, like the rings surrounding Saturn. (The diagram's not to scale, incidentally: it's just there to help you visualise what's going on.)

Around the actual cylinder you'll find a zone 20 kilometres ($12\frac{1}{2}$ miles) wide where spacetime is so brutally distorted that you couldn't exist there for so much as an instant, assuming you could get in there in the first place – most scientists are certain you couldn't since the very nature of the zone would fling your ship away before it could cross the boundary. On the diagram it's labelled as the Deadly Zone, for obvious reasons.

Outside the Deadly Zone, things start to get interesting. The next ring, labelled as the Zone of Time Reversal, is an area where time runs backwards. The outermost zone (Zone of Positive Time) brings you to a place where the flow of time will carry you into the future. Between the two is a Null Time Zone where interaction between positive and negative time flows produces an area where time (literally) stands still.

Beyond all the zones lies spacetime as we know it. That's where you'll lurk in your spaceship, trying to make up your mind when to go – forward to the future, backwards to the past. And whichever *when* you choose, you can take the trip secure in the knowledge that the closed timelike-lines of Tipler's mighty cylinder are there to bring you home again.

Chapter 21

Time Travellers

In the days when Professor Stephen Hawking was feeling pessimistic about time travel, he used to ask why, if such a thing were possible, we weren't flooded with time tourists from the future eager to experience the delights of the exotic 20th century. But this assumed that any method of time travel that might be developed would be safe, economical, legal, and suitable for everybody who wanted it. And why with the whole of time to pick from would time travellers be particularly interested in our era ... or even knew when to find it.

It is, of course, perfectly possible to imagine a method of time travel equivalent to a manned Mars probe today: dangerous and hideously expensive. Humanity might try it once or twice, but probably not often and only with small, courageous, well-trained crews. It's also possible to imagine time travel so appealing and addictive that the government of the day would outlaw it as quickly as such drugs as heroin or crack. Or the method of time travel might only work for women 25 years old at the peak of human fitness, or rely on some weird, physical abnormality present in 0.0001% of the population.

Factors like these – and it's possible to imagine many, many more – would reduce Professor Hawking's flood of time tourists to a trickle... which might find far more interesting events to witness (the destruction of the dinosaurs, the sinking of Atlantis) than anything available in our time. There's also the distinct possibility you might not recognise a time

traveller if one bit you on the backside. Would you even recognise what kind of vessel they would arrive in?

Physicists have done their calculations. They have worked out that if you were time travelling using a machine such as a Tipler cylinder – a conventional vessel, like the space shuttle used by NASA, wouldn't do. You would need something far smaller and more manoeuvrable, something that could switch direction instantly if it hit gravitational turbulence, something that could screen out the effects of G-force, maybe even of gravity itself, on its passengers. The physicists came up with the safest and most efficient design for a Tipler timeship. It would be shaped like a disc, flattened at the edges, bulging in the middle. In other words, it would look exactly like a flying saucer.

The modern history of flying saucers is usually dated back to 1947 when an American pilot named Kenneth Arnold saw nine of them over Mount Rainier in Washington State[7]. But the saucers had actually been showing up long before that. There are prehistoric rock paintings of flying saucers in Africa.

[7] For an in-depth look at the whole flying saucer phenomenon, read my *The Aliens Handbook*, published by Faber and Faber, 2005.

The Vedic texts of India are packed with flying saucer accounts: the ancient name for them was *vimanas.* Western experts date these texts to between 1500 and 1200 BC, but Indian scholars generally consider them much older – anywhere between 3500 and 3000 BC Both believe the written Vedas reflect a more ancient spoken tradition and some sources insist the events they record occurred *millions* of years ago.

In the writings of Ancient China, bright sky-discs were referred to as 'fiery dragons' and their movements carefully recorded. The Chinese believed they followed energy lines in the Earth (known as *lung-mei* or 'dragon paths') and that only emperors might be buried beneath one.

Egyptian scribes from the time of Tuthmoses III (15th century BC) recorded a virtual flying saucer invasion involving scores, perhaps hundreds, of craft witnessed by the Pharaoh himself and his nervous army.

Roman historians – notably Pliny – wrote of 'flying shields,' saucer-like aerial objects that sometimes accompanied great events like

Hannibal's crossing of the Alps. These sightings were so frequent that they eventually came to be looked on as omens – signs or warnings that a dramatic event was about to occur.

Flying saucers continued to appear long after the fall of Rome. Prints dating from the Middle Ages show panic in European cities caused by discs in the sky. There's even a 14th century fresco in an eastern European church that shows little men in space capsules cheerfully chugging along above our world. An early 17th century history book published in Switzerland, records the appearance of a spaceship over Arabia in 1479.

The sightings continued, century by century. There were saucers over Worcester, England in 1661, over Lisbon, the capital of Portugal, in 1755, over Magdeburg, Germany in 1802, over Cherbourg, France, several nights running in 1905. There were saucer sightings in America long before Kenneth Arnold filed his famous report which related how several discs flew over North Carolina from 1923 to 1926.

During the Second World War, Allied pilots often

returned from missions claiming they had been buzzed by 'foo-fighters' – small, saucer-shaped aircraft generally believed to be of German origin and, since they never attacked, possibly developed as spy planes. When the war ended, however, captured documents showed German *Luftwaffe* pilots had also been trailed by the saucers ... which the Nazis firmly believed were Allied aircraft.

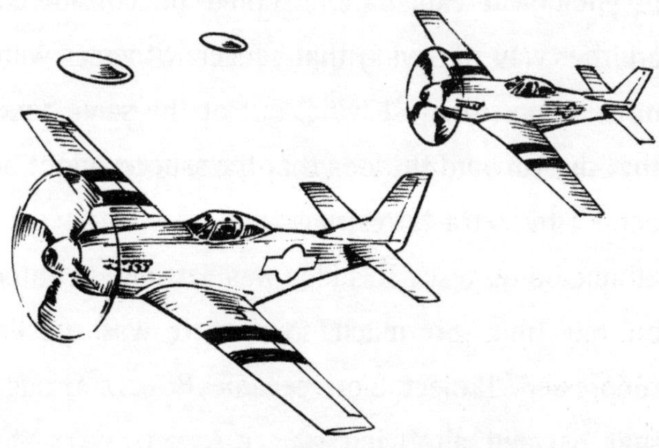

After the war, the American Government began to take flying saucers very seriously. Within three months of Kenneth Arnold's sighting, the Chief of Staff of the US Army and Commanding General of the Army Air Force recommended the formation of a study group to investigate the problem. The

investigation he recommended was actually set up and code named Project Sign. It came to the extraordinary conclusion that as little as possible should be done to investigate the saucers until it was shown they *weren't* a threat – after which they shouldn't be investigated at all.

Two members of the investigating team thought the existence of saucers was so unlikely that a psychological explanation should be considered; another way of saying that saucer witnesses were nuts, or possibly just lying. But at the same time, they put forward the idea that the saucers might be piloted by extra-terrestrials that were alarmed by atomic bomb tests. This idea was destined to catch on big time. So much so that it was quickly suppressed. Project Sign became Project Grudge that decided all flying saucer reports were the result of mistakes, mass hysteria, lying or mental illness.

It didn't work. In the years ahead, more and more people reported seeing flying saucers, including more than 12% of professional astronomers and two American Presidents (Ronald Reagan and

Jimmy Carter). A survey showed 61% of engineers and scientists believed flying saucers really existed and 8% had actually seen one. Some 40% admitted they believed them to be craft that came from outer space. It's probably fair to say that today, with saucer sightings a regular occurrence, most people think exactly the same thing. The question is, are they right?

Chapter 22

The Shape of Things to Come?

If you read flying saucer reports carefully, you'll quickly notice they have all the characteristics you'd expect from a timeship using some high-gravity device like a Tipler Cylinder. Remember what I said about timeships in the last chapter – you'd need something smaller and more manoeuvrable than our present spaceships, something that could switch direction instantly if it hit gravitational turbulence, something that could screen out the effects of G-force, maybe even of gravity itself, on its passengers.

Saucers tend to be a lot smaller than the NASA spaceships. As an American Army Air Force General noted, most of them are about the size of

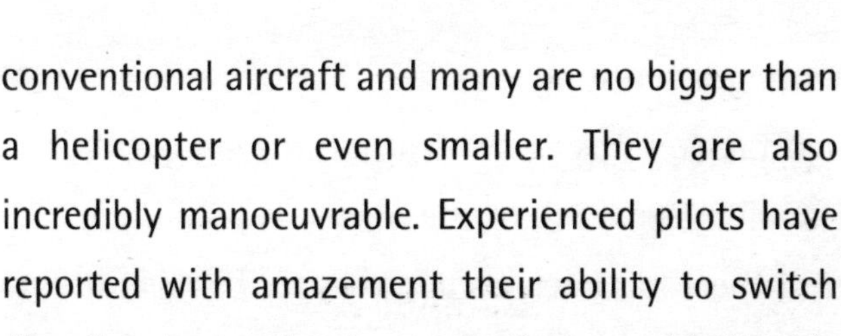

conventional aircraft and many are no bigger than a helicopter or even smaller. They are also incredibly manoeuvrable. Experienced pilots have reported with amazement their ability to switch direction instantly at speeds that would literally kill a human.

This is, in fact, one of the most tricky aspects of the whole flying saucer phenomenon. In the early days, it led scientists to believe the saucers couldn't possibly be solid or that witnesses were mistaken. Later, when the evidence for real, radar-reflecting saucers became overwhelming, the theory was developed that these had to be remote-controlled craft without living pilots.

Later still, as more and more witnesses insisted the saucers *did* have living pilots, Ufologists reluctantly began to conclude that the devices were engineered to shield their occupants from the gravitational forces generated by the high speed twists and turns.

So saucers have the right shape to be timeships and the right engineering to be timeships. They also, in many instances, *behave like* timeships,

visiting interesting eras like that of Ancient Egypt and taking ringside seats at interesting events, like Hannibal's crossing of the Alps. It is also interesting that there has been no alien-visitor behaviour – no landings on the White House lawn, no 'take me to your leader,' no mass communications, no interference with world events. They seem to be as careful *not* to interfere as the calmer members of the Time Safaris expedition in chapter 1. But what makes it really unlikely for these ships to be alien visitors seems to be the reports claiming flying saucers have crews – and these crews, in the vast majority of cases, are humanoid.

In the good old days of pulp magazine science fiction, extra-terrestrials were generally shown as green blobs with tentacles or giant insects.

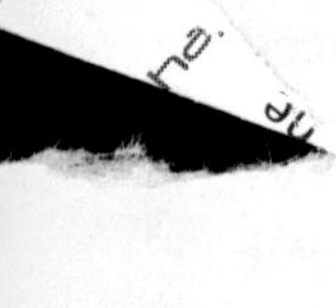

There was a very good reason for this: the chances against an alien planet evolving a life-form remotely resembling humanity are literally astronomical. Television series like *Star Trek* introduced a whole host of humanoid aliens – Klingons, Vulcans, Cardassians, Romulans, Ferengi – but the reason for that was largely cost. It's a lot cheaper to make up a human actor to look like a Klingon or Vulcan than it is to create the sort of realistic alien you find in Hollywood movies like ... well, *Alien*.

Yet outside of fiction, the vast majority of flying saucer occupants stand upright on two legs, have two arms, hands, fingers, head, eyes, nose, mouth and, sometimes, ears ... just like you and I. Have a look at these sample reports:

The beings had large, oval heads, greenish skin-tight clothing, long, thin limbs and webbed, three-fingered hands. Their eyes were large and oval with large, black pupils, their mouths seemed to consist of a small slit and their noses seemed to consist simply of two holes. (From, *Alien Identities,* by Richard L. Thompson)

As I approached him, a strange feeling came upon me... Outwardly there was no reason for this feeling for the man looked like any other man and I could see he was somewhat smaller than I and considerably younger. There were only two outstanding differences that I noticed as I neared him... His trousers were not like mine... His hair was long, reaching to his shoulders... (From *Flying Saucers Have Landed,* by Desmond Leslie and George Adamski)

Five humanoids passed through the closed front door of the house and came into the kitchen. They were ... small in stature, with large heads and large eyes. (From *Human Devolution* by Michael A. Cremo)

They appear as tall or short luminous entities... Reptilian creatures have been seen that seem to be carrying out mechanical functions... But by far the most common ... are the small 'grays', humanoid beings three or four feet (about 1 metre) in height. (They) have large, pear-shaped heads that protrude in the back, long arms and three or four long fingers, a thin torso and spindly legs... The beings are hairless with no ears, have rudimentary nostril holes and a thin slit for a mouth... By far the most prominent features are huge black eyes which curve upwards... (From *Abduction* by John E. Mack)

But if their looks might make you suspect that these are not aliens, their actions are guaranteed to send your suspicions off the scale.

Chapter 23

Alien Actions

There seems to be very little doubt that humanoid 'aliens' really do turn up from time to time, however difficult this is for many to accept. It is also not true that they only appear to lone individuals whose reports may just be descriptions of dreams or hallucinations.

In August, 1967, for example, two French children spotted four small humanoids standing beside a bright metallic sphere that had landed on the other side of a country road. The humanoids shone a bright light at the children, then floated up into the air and dived head-first into the sphere, which took off with a hissing sound and a distinct smell of sulphur.

It all seemed extremely unlikely, but a French government department mounted an investigation which backed up everything the youngsters had said. A *gendarme* (French policeman) arrived on the scene and confirmed there was a strong smell of sulphur. He also found tracks on the ground where the sphere had landed. A witness in the area said he'd heard the hissing sound.

The children's father, a respected member of their village community (he was actually Mayor) said they had both smelled of sulphur after the incident and their eyes were running for days. This was confirmed by the local doctor who examined them.

The investigating judge eventually concluded, 'There is no flaw or inconsistency ... that permit us to doubt the sincerity of the witnesses or to reasonably suspect an invention, hoax or hallucination. Under these circumstances, despite the young age of the principal witnesses and as extraordinary as the facts... seem to be, I think that they actually observed them.'

An even more solidly confirmed case occurred in the United States in 1975. A 72-year-old businessman named George O'Barski was driving

home to New Jersey from his shop on Manhattan Island in New York City. He'd reached North Hudson Park about one or two in the morning when a shining saucer flew over his car with a loud humming noise and landed in a park a little way ahead. The vehicle was about 9 metres long with narrow glowing windows. While it hovered some metres above the ground, a door opened in the side and several small helmeted humanoids emerged.

The creatures dug up some earth and took it back to their craft, which rose directly upwards, then flew off towards the north. An astounded O'Barski drove on home, but returned to the site the following day and discovered the holes left by these bizarre visitors. If anything, this close encounter seemed even more unlikely than the French case. But when it was professionally investigated, it soon turned out Mr O'Barski wasn't the only one to see the saucer. A doorman at an apartment complex near the park spotted it in the small hours of the same January night. Like O'Barski, he described it as having lighted windows and floating about 3 metres above the ground. The doorman was so intrigued that he mentioned it to a police lieutenant who lived in the building – something confirmed by the officer himself. A second doorman came forward to say he'd seen the same object at the same place six days previously.

A family named Wamsley also came forward. They lived some 14 blocks away from the apartment building, but their home was on the flight path O'Barski said the object had taken when it left the park. Late on the January night in question, a son of the family, 12-year-old Robert, saw the saucer through his window. He immediately alerted other family members who went outside and watched the craft for two minutes as it moved slowly away.

Investigations like these – just two of many – confirm the physical reality of the saucers and their little humanoid occupants. And what they get up to is very strange indeed. The experience of an American called Peter is fairly typical. While in the Caribbean during 1987–1988 he woke up in the night to find small, hooded humanoids in his room. He shouted at them, but they brought him outside to a brightly lit patio where he was transported into a flying saucer hovering above the treetops.

This was the first of several abductions during which the little humanoids somehow took control of his will and his feelings, leaving him docile and sometimes even paralysed. In this state he was carefully examined and some sort of hand-held device used to dampen his fear reactions.

He was stretched out on a tilted examination table and probed using something he described as a 'dentist's ... instrument.' The probe went through his skin and all the way into his abdomen, although without causing any pain.

Then they inserted a tube through his anus to take a stool sample and leave some sort of implant – he thought it might be an information chip – inside his bowel. Afterwards he told Professor Mack, 'I feel like a tagged animal...'

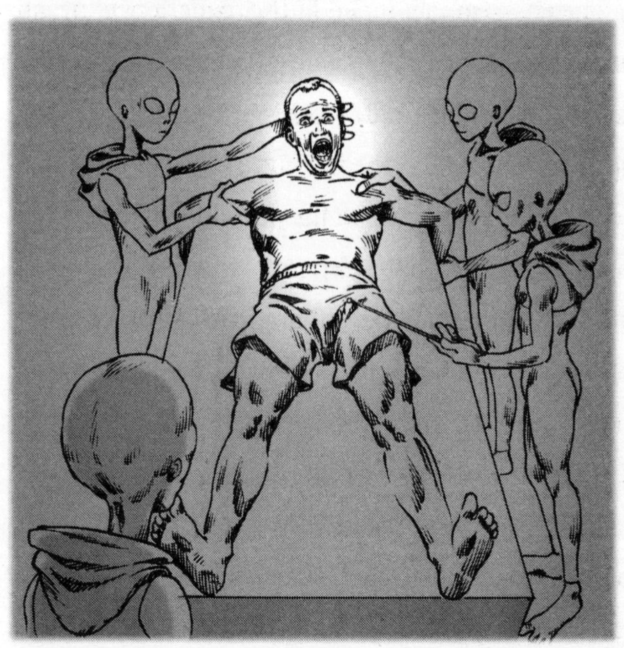

On another occasion, the creatures inserted a probe at the corner of his left eye and used it to extract something from his brain – he thought it might be an implant from a previous abduction. On yet another they drilled into his nose and left something in it.

In his book about abduction experiences, Professor Mack reported that abductees frequently felt that some sort of homing device had been inserted into their bodies – usually but not always the head – so that the humanoids could track them, in much the same way as naturalists tag wild animals with tiny radio transmitters in order to keep track of where they are.

The implants aren't imagination. Several have been recovered and subjected to rigorous tests. These showed no signs of rare metals or unusual combinations of common metals. One that came out of a woman abductee's nose was a twisted fibre of carbon, silicon, oxygen and various trace elements. The only thing the scientists could say about it was that it was 'not a naturally occurring biological object,' in other words, not something

that had grown there, like a wart.

If you take an average abduction case, there's a clear pattern of what's likely to happen: the victims are usually undressed and forced onto an examination table, sometimes alone, sometimes with a whole room-full of others undergoing a similar procedure. They are then visually examined, often at very close range with the little humanoids' eyes only a few centimetres or so away from their skin. Skin, hair and internal body samples are taken using surgical instruments that are sometimes extremely painful. Apart from samples, instruments are used to penetrate just about every part of the body, but most usually the head. For some reason the chest is not usually touched.

The humanoids seem to be particularly interested in human reproduction. Sperm samples are often taken from men, eggs from women. Many female abductees have reported being made pregnant by the humanoids and later abducted again to have the baby removed.

Cases like these strongly suggest there's some sort of breeding programme being carried out. The

visitors are clearly interested both in fully human and cross-bred children. Sometimes mothers are shown incubators where babies are being raised and are encouraged by the humanoids to hold and nurture them.

Alongside the examinations, there is also very often what appears to be some sort of telepathic contact. During this the victim is fed information on the fate of the planet and the responsibility humans bear for many of its problems. Images shown include pollution, nuclear war, earthquakes, firestorms and floods.

When the whole process – physical and mental – is finished, the victims usually forget their experiences, at least for a while. Later the memories can emerge naturally, piece by piece, sometimes when awake, sometimes in dreams. Flying saucer investigators frequently try to speed up the process by using hypnosis.

All this is very creepy, but does it really add up, as many people believe, to aliens visiting our planet? A friend of mine, who dismisses all flying saucer reports as nonsense, once remarked, 'I can't imagine why an alien species should travel millions of miles through the depths of space just to stick a probe up my bottom.'

There are, in fact, many problems with the idea that flying saucers arrived from Outer Space. Why should aliens come here at all? Why should they be interested in the fate of our planet? The idea that aliens can interbreed with humans is roughly equivalent to suggesting a giraffe might mate with a bluebottle.

And while the scientists insist the humanoid shape is so unlikely to develop on another planet that you might as well forget it, we know – because we live here – that it actually did develop on Earth. Thus, if you see a humanoid, you can be reasonably certain he or she (or possibly it) is an Earth-based lifeform.

Since the majority of saucer pilots clearly aren't lifeforms that are sharing the world with us today, you could wonder if they might be lifeforms that occupy our world tomorrow. You might even put forward the theory that they are our distant descendants.

The little 'grays' humanoids fit this idea rather well. The theory of evolution suggests that species change to adapt to their environment. You might argue that with the coming of a technical, computerised civilisation, the need for big, strong, muscular bodies will grow less and less.

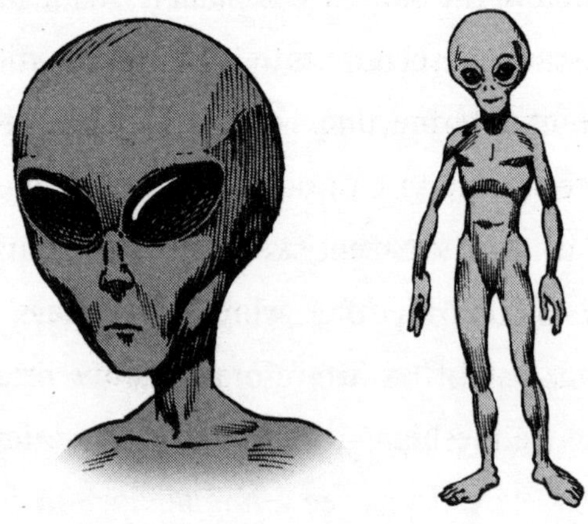

As machines do more and more, you might expect us to get smaller, with more spindly limbs. And since intelligence becomes increasingly important, if only to keep up with the machines, you might expect brains to enlarge and heads, consequently, to expand. If the Sun dimmed in a few million years, or the Earth grew dark for any other reason – pollution of the atmosphere comes to mind – it would make sense for our species to develop large, nocturnal eyes.

Visitors of this sort would have a keen interest in their human past, would be concerned with such issues as nuclear warfare and the greenhouse effect, would use probes manufactured from commonplace elements. As our distant descendants, they would still be capable of interbreeding with us. They would be interested in the fate of our planet. They might be driven by a desire to tinker with the course of human history. In other words, the 'grays' look suspiciously like the future of humanity, returned in their timeships to study their primitive ancestors.

Chapter 24

Ancient Finds

There are, in fact, reasonable explanations of the flying saucer phenomenon that don't involve time travel. But even if the saucers haven't flown through time, there's still evidence that time travel has 'already' happened.[8] Let's start with William Meister.

William J. Meister isn't a time traveller – he's an American, a draftsman by profession – but he is and always has been interested in the past. His major hobby is collecting fossil trilobites. Trilobites look much like very tiny lobsters, which is more or less what they were. They swarmed in their thousands in the warm, shallow seas that covered the Earth when our planet was young. They've been extinct now for millions of years.

Back in 1968, Mr Meister took advantage of the

[8] Or will happen. Or will have happened. Getting your tenses sorted when you're writing about time is very tricky.

pleasant summer weather to go fossil hunting in Utah, USA. During the course of the afternoon he split open a block of shale which, it turned out, did contain trilobite remains. But the creatures seemed to have been crushed by a human foot. They were embedded in the fossil of a perfect shoeprint. In size and shape it was in almost every way exactly like a modern shoe, the sort you'd wear to go to school. All the signs are it came off somebody's right foot. The rock that held it was once on the surface of the Earth and is somewhere between 500 and 600 million years old.

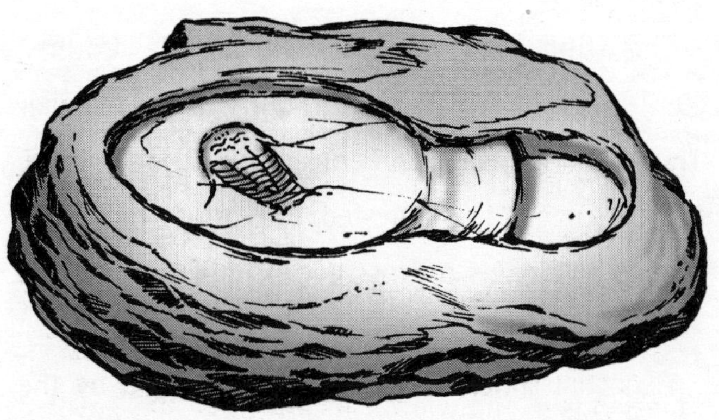

Meister's find is just one of several similar discoveries. In 1938, for example, Professor W. G.

Burroughs, who was then head of the Department of Geology at Berea College, Kentucky, USA, reported the discovery of what looked like footprints sunk into the horizontal surface of an outcrop of hard massive grey sandstone.

There were three pairs of tracks, showing left and right footprints. The toes were spread apart like those of somebody used to walking barefoot. The foot was curved like your foot and had a heel like your heel. In some of the tracks you could see the imprints of left and right feet. The distance between them was just what you'd expect in human footprints.

This find was made at Rockcastle County, Kentucky, but Professor Burroughs claimed similar tracks had appeared in Pennsylvania and Missouri. When somebody suggested the prints had been carved by Indians, microscopic examination showed they were genuine fossils.

A partial shoeprint was found fossilised by the geologist John T. Reid in Nevada. Although the front part was missing, some two-thirds of the print remained intact – enough to show the

threadwork that was sewed on the sole. Microscopic examination showed the thread twist, proving the shoe sole was man-made. Analysis of the rock placed it in the Triassic Era, dating the fossil to between 213 and 248 million years ago.

Fossil human footprints have also been found in and around the Paluxy River, near Glen Rose in Texas. Dinosaur footprints were found in the same strata. In 1983, a fossilised human footprint was found next to the fossil footprint of a three-toed

dinosaur in the Turkmen Republic, part of what was then the southwestern U.S.S.R. Dinosaurs became extinct 96 million years ago.

In 1928, a coalminer named Atlas A. Mathis was working in a 3-kilometre (2-mile) deep shaft in Oklahoma when blasting operations unearthed several 30-centimetre concrete cubes, polished to a mirror finish on all sides. These turned out to be part of a well-built wall that ran underground for 100 metres or more.

More than 50 years earlier, there were reports of a slate wall in an Ohio coalmine that bore several lines of hieroglyphs carved in bold relief. Most coal in America dates to the Carboniferous Era, which would make these walls more than 286 million years old.

During the late 1960s, quarrying work at Saint-Jean de Livet in France unearthed an ancient chalk bed, estimated to be some 65 million years old. Inside it were several manufactured metal tubes, all somewhat oval in shape, but varying in size.

In 1891, Mrs. S. W. Culp, an Illinois housewife, was breaking up a large piece of coal that wouldn't fit in her scuttle when an eight-carat, 25-centimetre-long gold chain fell out. When she first saw it, Mrs. Culp assumed the chain had been dropped into her coal bunker, but then noticed the two ends of the chain were still embedded in the lump she'd just broken. Hollows in each half showed where the chain itself had rested. The coal Mrs. Culp was using came from a mine in south Illinois and was somewhere between 260 and 320 million years old.

There was an earlier echo of Mrs Culp's find in 1844 when workmen quarrying rock near the River Tweed in England discovered a length of gold thread embedded in stone at a depth of just under 3 metres. The stone was between 320 and 360 million years old.

In the same year, a metal nail turned up

embedded (head and all) in a block of sandstone from a quarry at Mylnfield in the north of England. It was discovered when the stone was being prepared for use in building. The stone itself was between 360 and 408 million years old.

What have these finds got to do with time travel? To answer that question, you need to know something about the history of life on this planet.

Chapter 25

Signs of the Times

The dinosaurs were wiped out – most scientists now think by the impact of a massive lump of rock from space – some 96 million years ago. Before that, the only mammal species on the planet was a little tree shrew too small to attract much attention. Mammals hadn't a hope of spreading while the saurians were about, but the violent death of the dinosaurs was a chance for the tree shrew.

Although some scientists think our entire planet rang like a gong when the asteroid struck, it wasn't impact-blast that did for the dinosaurs. What happened was that the explosion threw enormous quantities of dust and debris into our atmosphere, blocking out the Sun.

Without sunlight, plants withered and died. With

vast areas of vegetation gone, the animals that fed off it gradually starved. Then the meat-eaters, like *Tyrannosaurus rex*, ran out of prey and they starved as well.

It was a slow, painful process and you don't have to be a rocket scientist to work out that the big eaters, the massive dinosaurs, fell over first. The little tree shrew, our world's first mammal, wasn't a big eater. A leaf or two and a few nuts might have kept her going for weeks. She hung in there, eating this and that, until the sun came out again.

The Sun came out on a very changed world. Vegetation recovered, of course: seeds can lie waiting to grow for centuries, even millennia. But the dinosaurs and many other ancient species were gone. There was nobody left to terrorise our little tree shrew. She came down to the plains, ate her fill without worry for the first time in her timid life, and began to reproduce like crazy.

Over millions of years, random mutations (random changes) and natural selection (the process whereby living things adapt to their environment) transformed that little tree shrew into every mammal species on the planet. And one of those species was us. All this happened *after* the big extinction 96 million years ago. It could not have happened before then, because conditions simply would not allow it.

So what made all those human footprints that date to the age of the dinosaurs? According to some scientists they aren't human footprints at all: they only *look* like human footprints. They are, in fact, the footprints of a wholly unknown species of dinosaur, no other traces of which have ever been

found by anybody anywhere, that just happened to walk upright on two legs with a stride identical to a grown man and five-toed feet that were shaped exactly like ours.

Which is all very fine until you ask which breed of dinosaur was known for wearing shoes. But shoeprints aside, something intelligent was wandering the Earth long before the dinosaurs died out. Something that built walls, manufactured metal tubes, used nails, gold thread and gold chains. Whatever it was seems to have been around for a very long time. Hundreds of manufactured metal spheres, each about the size of a cricket ball and some with parallel grooves cut round their middles, have been unearthed by miners in South Africa's Western Transvaal. They are almost 3,000 million years old.

Since the Earth itself is thought to be only a little more than 4,000 million years old, you have to ask yourself what the planet was like when the spheres were first dropped in South Africa. Scientists frankly aren't too sure – there are almost no fossils from the period. But they think the Earth had an atmosphere, maybe even one we could breathe: a mix of nitrogen, carbon dioxide, water vapour and oxygen. There was no such place as South Africa, no such place as Africa itself. The landmasses formed vast supercontinents which only broke apart many millions of years later to form the continents we know today.

The place wasn't exactly teeming with life – at least not life you would notice. There was some bacteria and a little algae on the surface of the shallow rock pools. There were no animals, of any sort, on land, no fish in the sea. So far geologists have unearthed only the faintest traces of 'a soft-bodied, multicellular organism. In other words, the spheres date to a time when, scientists believe, the most advanced form of life on our planet was some sort of slime mould.

Is it possible the spheres came down from Outer Space? Did a vessel from Sirius or Alpha Centauri pull into our solar system all those ages ago and dump some ballast, in the form of metal spheres, on a newly formed planet orbiting third from the Sun? Perhaps this did happen, but frankly there is no way of telling for sure whether the mystery spheres are of alien origin. But the carved stone found in a coal mine near Webster, Iowa, is definitely the work of humanity: it bears humanity's face.

In 1897, a miner working at a depth of about 40 metres unearthed a dark grey piece of stone (usually identified as slate) about 30 centimetres long and 10 centimetres thick. Geometrical lines forming a pattern of diamonds were etched into the surface of the stone. Inside each diamond was an engraved drawing of an old man. Most of these portraits showed him looking to the right. In two he was looking left. The stone is somewhere between 286 and 360 million years old.

The inlaid metal vase found at Dorchester, Massachusetts, in 1852, was also clearly of human

manufacture. This bell-shaped vessel was blown out of solid rock during blasting operations at Meeting House Hill. The blast broke it in two. When the pieces were put together, the 10.5 centimetre-high vase, tapering from base to top, showed itself to be inlaid with flowers and vines, delicately wrought in silver. This attractive artefact is 600 million years old.

But the proof that men walked the Earth long before the death of the dinosaurs does not rely on any of the evidence already quoted, however compelling that evidence might be. The proof arose in 1862 when, according to a contemporary

report, the skeleton of a man was discovered 30 metres below the surface of the earth in a coal-bed capped by 60 centimetres of slate.

When first found the bones were encrusted in some glossy black material, but showed white when scraped. They are at least 286 million years old. They may be as much as 320 million years old.

Bearing in mind that modern humans are supposed to have first appeared in Africa no longer than 200,000 years ago, quite a few modern skeletons have turned up in archaeological strata that show at least a few people were wandering the planet at a much earlier period.

Twelve million year old bones have turned up in Argentina, along with clear signs somebody had made a fire. Bones of a similar age were discovered in France. A human skeleton that's somewhere between 33 and 35 million years old was unearthed in Table Mountain in California. Another, found at Delémont, in Switzerland, is even older – between 38 and 35 million years.

Human remains dated at a million years or more have been found in Argentina, South Africa, Java,

Tanzania, Italy, Kenya, China, Belgium, North America, England and Greece. When you add in other signs of human habitation – hearths, beads, decorated shells, trenchwork and the like – the list of countries expands dramatically. What on Earth is happening here? Why is there so much hard evidence of human activity on our planet millions of years before the first human ever evolved?

Well, it could be the scientists have simply got it wrong – I'd be the last one to argue scientists never make mistakes. It could be humanity appeared on this planet hundreds of millions of years ago, perhaps even springing up miraculously before the poor old slime mould got going. Or it could be that what we're seeing here is litter – the litter of time travellers from our distant future who left signs of their presence in manufactured items like the metal spheres, in artworks like the vase and inscribed slate, in items like the embedded nail, in decorative objects like the gold chain and thread.

Perhaps, like modern campers, some of these time travellers enjoyed living rough and so built

fires to preserve the batteries of their heaters. Perhaps some of them liked the simpler life on an unpolluted planet where a man could admire clear skies and avoid the ravages of pollution. Perhaps some stayed and built sturdy stone and concrete walls to keep out the dinosaurs. And perhaps some died, through accident or old age, leaving their bleached bones to puzzle the archaeologists of our present age – time travellers of tomorrow who enjoyed their last years yesterday.

Chapter 26

The Day After Tomorrow

So, is time travel really possible? The great British physicist, Stephen Hawking, used to say no. Now he's changed his mind. He's come to the conclusion that there's nothing in modern scientific thought to prove you *can't* travel in time and some findings suggest you *can.*

To follow his reasoning, you'd need to be a lot better at maths than I am, but it's possible to answer our basic question without using maths at all. Start with something familiar – the way you get about in space. When you walk from here to there, you know perfectly well there's no law of nature that says you can't walk back again. But when you travel from today to tomorrow, you know with absolute certainty you'll never be able to make the return trip.

Yet that conviction is only based on past experience. The equations of motion worked out by Newton show clearly that you *should* be able to come back from tomorrow – and that discovery is supported both by Relativity Theory and the findings of Quantum Physics (the study of atomic particles).

Thus we can say with confidence that time travel really is possible: it's just that we can't do it. But even that isn't true, because quite clearly there are people who *did* do it, even though, in most cases, they hadn't the least idea how.

The trick, of course, will be discovering some way – maybe by inventing an ingenious machine, maybe by developing a rigorous training programme – that allows anyone to take safe, economical and pleasant time trips whenever the fancy takes them. We haven't managed that trick just yet, but there is evidence to suggest we will definitely get the hang of it one day.

When that day comes, we'll walk with dinosaurs and discover what awaits us the day after tomorrow.

Further reading

All the books in the *Forbidden Truths* series have been the result of careful, wide-ranging research, but they aren't the last word about anything. You're the only person in the world who can decide what's true and what's not, so you might want to do a little further research for yourself. I found the following list of books helpful in writing this one. You might like to dip into one or two of them yourself. And while I think of it, the following website will prove interesting: http://freespace.virgin.net/steve.preston/Time.html.

Alien Identities, Richard L. Thompson, Govardhan Hill Inc, Alachua, Florida, 1995.

A Study of History, Arnold Toynbee, Oxford University Press, 1954.

An Experiment with Time, J. W. Dunne, Faber and Faber, London, 1958.

Arthur C. Clarke's Mysterious World, Simon Welfare and John Fairley, Fontana Books, London, 1982.

Black Holes: the End of the Universe? John Taylor, Souvenir Press, London, 1973.

Chaos, James Gleick, Cardinal, London, 1988.

Encounters with the Unknown, Colin Parsons, Robert Hale Ltd., London, 1990.

Flying Saucers Through the Ages, Paul Thomas, Tandem, London, 1973.

Forbidden Archaeology, by Michael A. Cremo and Richard L. Thompson, Bhaktivedanta Institude, San Diego, 1993.

Mysteries, Colin Wilson, Panther Books, London, 1979.

Mysteries of the Unexplained, Carroll C. Calkins (ed.) Reader's Digest Books, London, 1982.

Nostradamus, Visions of the Future, J. H. Brennan, Aquarian Press, London, 1993.

Parallel Universes, Fred Alan Wolf, Touchstone Books, New York.

Premonitions: a Leap into the Future, Herbert B. Greenhouse, Bernard Geis Associates, 1972.

The Arrow of Time, Peter Coveney and Roger Highfield, Flamingo Books, London, 1991.

The Occult, Colin Wilson, Grafton Books, London, 1989.

The Prophecies of Nostradamus, Erika Chetham, Corgi Books, London, 1989.

The UFO Experience, J. Allen Hynek, Corgi Books, London, 1974.

Index